DAUGHTER OF HADES
ENCHANTED

BOOK FOUR

Foxtales Press

DANI HOOTS

COPYRIGHT

Enchanted

Daughter of Hades, #4

© 2020 FoxTales Press

Content edits by Justin Boyer

Proofreading by Victory Editing

Cover Design Copyright © 2020 by Biserka Designs

All rights reserved.

This is a work of fiction. All characters and events portrayed in this novel are fictitious and are products of the author's imagination. Any resemblance to actual events, locales, or persons, living or dead, is entirely coincidental.

ISBN for paperback: 978-1-942023-73-9

ISBN for hardcover: 978-1-942023-74-6

CHAPTER 1

Chrys

The salty scent of the ocean filled my nostrils as a warm breeze caressed my skin.

My eyes batted open, and I found myself in a quaint room. The walls were made of a light wood, and nothing decorated the area except the single bed I found myself on, an end table, a dresser, and a chair on the other side of the room where a man sat. He had his red-haired head leaned against the wall, eyes shut. I didn't say anything quite yet, as I didn't know who he was or what I was doing there.

The aroma of the ocean came in from an open window, and the white curtains danced in the air. I would have found it quite relaxing if I'd known why the hell I found myself there.

Or who the hell I was.

The man stirred and his eyes opened. I stared at him and quickly sat upright in my bed, not sure what to say. Once he saw me, he jumped up, causing me to clutch the blue quilt.

He approached me and I shrank back even more. He stopped, noticing my fear.

"You're awake! Are you okay? How are you feeling?"

I glanced around. I didn't know if there were others in the house, but so far no one else had approached the room. "I… I don't know. Who are you? Where am I? Who… am I?"

I found it strange that his eyes seemed to flicker with happiness. He looked down at his hands. "There… there was an accident. You were attacked by a god by the name of Zeus. He thinks you are a threat and wants you dead. You didn't do anything, but luckily a couple of us were able to get you out of there, but not before he wiped your memories."

"I'm… a goddess?" I asked.

He nodded. "Yes, one who is most powerful. We brought you somewhere where he will never find you and where we can train your powers and keep you safe. Then, when the time is right, you can defeat him."

That was a lot to process. I was a goddess and needed

to learn to use my powers to kill another god? Was that even possible? What powers did I posses? It felt somewhat right, but I knew there was still something missing. "But… but I don't know who I am. Everything feels new to me. How can I trust what you are saying is true?"

"You are Papavera, but most people call you Vera. And you can believe me because I am your father."

I tried to sort through any memories I had, but everything was a blank. I didn't feel any attachment to the name, nor this man, but neither did it feel wrong.

Then my head started to hurt.

I placed my hand on my head. "I… I don't know what to think. This is a lot to take in. If you are telling the truth and I am your daughter, please tell me where we are."

"You are on Aeaea, which is an island under the protection of the goddess Circe. She will help us train you and has potions and herbal formulas that will help you regain your powers and some of your memories. But first you should rest. Then when you awaken, I will introduce you to the others."

The mention of herbal potions brought up an image of a teacup in my hand and a woman who smiled. That memory made my head hurt even more.

I nodded. "Yeah, that sounds good. I think I need more rest."

"Good night, my flower."

As he left, my heart started aching from the nickname he called me. Was it from a memory?

Lying back down, I tried to hold on to that word—to that image of a dark-haired man whose face was foggy and unrecognizable.

"My flower."

Before I knew it, I had dozed off once again.

The second time I awoke, the sun's light was just beginning to peek through my open window. Birds chirped in the distance, bringing me back to the world I had found myself in.

That's right. I couldn't remember anything.

At least I could remember that, I supposed. I got up, my legs wobbling a little. I wondered how long I had been asleep. After a moment, I was able to make my way to the dresser and open it up. Inside was filled with white sundresses and blue jeans. I grabbed one of each and put them on.

Glancing in the mirror, I felt off. This outfit… was it something I had worn before? It looked good on me I had to admit, but something seemed strange. Then again, everything was strange right now.

Taking a deep breath, I decided to venture into the rest of the house and see if I could find the man who'd said he was my father. Opening my door, I stepped into a hallway. I could hear voices to my right, so I decided to follow them.

As I ventured down the hallway, I was led into the living area and kitchen. A man and woman were sitting at the table, eating. When they saw me, they quickly got up.

"Vera, you are awake!" The man who called himself my father wrapped his arms around me. "I am so glad. The last time you woke up was over two days ago."

Had it really been that long? It felt like I had simply closed my eyes and opened them again. What had happened to cause this? Could Zeus really have knocked me out like that?

He backed away and gestured to a woman who had long, curly brown hair and green eyes. "This is Circe. She will be the one teaching you how to use your power. Both of us will be filling in the gaps that are missing from Zeus's attack."

"What about the other person you mentioned? You said there were a couple of others."

"Oh him…" My father bit his lip. "He's out. He has a lot of duties as a god, but don't worry. He will be back later, and I will introduce you to him."

Circe stepped up to me. "It is a pleasure to finally meet you."

"We haven't met before?" I asked.

She shook her head. "No, we have not, but I am an

old friend of your father's. It actually works out as no one will suspect you are here since it has been over a millennium since your father and I have talked."

"And you are willing to risk your life to help? Why?"

She laughed, and I found her voice to be quite sweet. "You are one suspicious girl."

"Well, since I don't remember anything, I feel I should be extra cautious."

"Oh, I didn't mean it as a bad thing. It's refreshing, as many don't question their surroundings." She gestured to the table. "Take a seat and I will make you some breakfast."

I did as she asked and sat next to my father. He squeezed my hand.

"I am so glad you are fine, my flower. I was so very worried."

His skin felt warm on my hand, but it didn't feel... real. Something was bothering me about him, and I couldn't place it. Perhaps it was just the side effects of the amnesia.

"I'm fine other than my memories. Do you believe I can get them back? What did Zeus do to me to make me forget everything?" I took in a deep breath.

"I am hoping Circe can make something that will help you remember, but it is going to take some time. As for Zeus, he used a poison from the Underworld called Lethe. Its use is for the dead to drink in order to forget their memories of their life so they can rest in peace."

Lethe. The Underworld. Both those words seemed to trigger something and caused my head to start aching again. I pressed my hand to my head.

"Oh, your headache again. Look, let's stay away from questions about the past for a moment. You seem to be hurting every time I bring it up."

I nodded. "Yeah, I think that is a good idea."

A few moments later, Circe brought in some breakfast. I stared at the feast in astonishment. The platter was covered in strawberries, orange slices, pears, grilled zucchini, carrots of all colors, cauliflower, slices of homemade bread, and what looked like a dozen boiled eggs.

"Eat to your heart's content. I'm sure you are starving after being asleep for so long."

My stomach grumbled in response, and both my father and Circe laughed. I felt my cheeks begin to blush as I filled my plate with a little of each of the contents on the platter. I took a bite of the thick toast and closed my eyes in bliss. It was warm and sweet.

"Here." Circe grabbed a pot. "Have some tea as well. It's a special blend that helps with memory. It has rosemary, gotu kola, ginkgo, and ashwagandha. Of course, we will also need some stronger magic, but this will be a good start for getting your brain working."

I nodded and took a sip. It was very pungent, but I didn't mind the taste. If it helped, I wouldn't complain. "Thank you."

"My pleasure. For the first few days, we will be taking it easy. Once I think you are well enough, we will use the stronger potions on you. I just want to make sure your body can handle it first."

I nodded, a little scared at what sort of potions she would be using. As I peered back down at the tea, I realized it felt familiar.

"Strange, I remember sitting and drinking tea like this with someone. I guess it had to be someone else if it wasn't you. Are there any other witch goddesses like you whom I interacted with before fighting Zeus?"

Circe and my father glanced at each other, a little bit of nervousness in their eyes. My father finally answered. "You have had many friends who drink tea. I'm not sure which one you are remembering."

I glanced back down at the tea, twirling it in the cup. "Ah. I guess that makes sense. A lot of people drink tea these days."

"That they do, all because I taught them about herbal medicine. If only humans actually showed me thanks. Most of them were slaughtered, however, in the name of a different god. And now they don't remember the wisdom I gave them. It is depressing to watch."

I wasn't sure what to say to that. She seemed sad, her

eyes looking down at her own cup. I decided to change the subject a little. "Father, what are you the god of?"

He smiled. "I am not a god but the Titan of Fire who goes by the name of Prometheus. I came along before the gods of Olympus, but they don't seem to care about that. Zeus thinks that since he is so powerful, he can rule over anyone and anything." He gently placed a loose strand of my brown hair behind my ear. "That is, until you came along, my dear flower. You are the one who can finally bring that monster down once and for all."

I gulped down the strawberry that was in my mouth. Was he speaking the truth? Was I really the one who would bring an end to Zeus? And what did that even entail?

Who exactly was I?

CHAPTER 2

Huntley

How could he betray us like that?

We were back in Pothos's flat. No one said anything —all mainly pissed off at what Prometheus had done. Hades stood in the corner, dark anger almost visibly pouring off him. Persephone sat in an overstuffed chair closest to him, holding her head in her hands. Pothos and Mel sat on the couch, also trying to think of what to do next.

I, of course, paced. No one made any comments to my having to move around as we all puzzled over just what we might have to do. It had only been a day since Prometheus and Apollo had kidnapped Chrys, although it felt like days had passed. Anger still swept over all of us, clouding our judgment.

Speaking of clouds, areas around the world were experiencing intense thunderstorms since yesterday. It was not only all over the news but also happening at the moment in London. I had never seen anything like it, and in any other circumstances, I would have thought it pretty cool.

This, however, was not a good circumstance. Zeus was angry and causing problems all over the world during his childish fit. I knew he didn't actually care about Chrys but was more acting out because he had been tricked and betrayed by Apollo. He was looking for Chrys as well, hoping these storms would draw them out.

We had to find Chrys before Zeus did—that much I knew. Not only for Chrys's safety but also so a war between Hades and Zeus didn't ensue, although I had a feeling no matter who found her first, it was going to turn into some kind of war. The storm outside did not help that sense of foreboding.

Another flash lit the dark sky outside, and the trailing thunder shook Pothos's flat. Pothos let out a brief sigh.

"I swear, if he targets this place, I'm going to be pissed. I've already had to fix so much because of this mess," he whispered.

Mel placed a hand on his back. "You know the gods never hold back. That's why we usually stay in the shadows."

He let out a little chuckle. "Yeah, I suppose you are right. And we are in this for the long run, so the question is, what do we do now?"

Hades was the first to answer. "We find Prometheus and Apollo and we kill them. Simple as that."

"Except we have to find them first." Persephone looked up, tears running down her face and ruining her makeup. "We don't even know where to start."

"We start from the beginning." Mel stood up and looked out the window. "Where would Prometheus take her? It would be somewhere remote—somewhere he can train her to use her powers."

Pothos let out a sigh. "Except there are so many places on this world where he could hide, as long as he really thought it out. There are so many caves, mountains, islands. Hell, he could be in some tunnel below London for all we know."

Persephone shook her head. "No, we also have to think about Apollo. It will be somewhere warm and with lots of sunlight. He can't stand caves or being underground."

"So an island. That has to narrow it down, right?" I asked. "How many islands can there really be?"

"Over a million uninhabited. Thousands in warm water."

I couldn't believe what I was hearing. Thousands?

There was no way we would be able to search all of these. Were there really that many? Hell, hearing that made me realize that Atlantis and all those mythical islands could be real without having been discovered by mortals.

"How will we search all the islands?" I asked. "Is there something we can do to speed up the process?"

Mel answered, "I think first we need to see what gods will help us. Then we can split up and eliminate Prometheus's hideouts first. He told me the location of a few of them, and I'm sure others know more."

Hades shook his head. "No god is going to help us right now, not with him"—he pointed up at the storm—"throwing around his power like this. This storm isn't just to find Apollo and Prometheus but a warning to all the gods who dare betray him. No, I doubt any god will help us."

"We can still try," Persephone said. "A few might…" She put her head back in her hands. "I just…"

Hades stepped forward and placed his hand on her back. "It's not your fault. Don't blame yourself."

"Yes it is! If I had been a better mother, none of this would have happened! I'm a failure as a mother!"

I wanted to help her, but truth be told, some of this was indirectly her fault. If she hadn't pushed Hades away like she did, Chrys would have never thought about leaving the Underworld to go see what the mortal realm was like.

A cough from the other side of the room grabbed our attention. AJ sat there, still bound to the wooden chair we had put him in.

"Not to interrupt, but you do realize if Prometheus took her to an island, they would be discovered quickly by my father. Poseidon is able to identify anything that is in the sea. So unless they were careful and made sure never to touch the water, I think an island might be unlikely."

Hades walked over to him and slapped him across the face with the back of his hand. The sound of the skin contacting skin was loud, and I couldn't imagine how painful it was. AJ's face was immediately red, and he appeared as if he was trying to hold back tears.

"Now," Hades said as he turned back to us. "Where were we?"

Everyone was silent after what he had done. Mel was the first to speak. "I think we need to make a list of places where he used to hide from Zeus and find other gods who might help us. Then we split up and start searching."

Hades nodded. "That sounds like a good idea. Anyone have a pen and paper?"

The list of hideouts was long. I mean, like, it was going to take us weeks even if we split up. Prometheus apparently liked to hide from Zeus quite often, which brought up more questions than answers. It made sense that he wanted Chrys to use her power to take down Zeus, but it didn't explain why he kidnapped her. If the marriage simply got canceled, why didn't he just talk her into it? I guess he wanted to ensure that she would listen to him and actually go after Zeus. Knowing Chrys, she probably would have just gone back to the Underworld with me and never leave again. There was no reason to start a fight if one could find happiness a different way.

Hades closed the pen. "Okay, so this is what we have: fifteen places to search and only five of us. For now."

Mel scanned the list. "Again, there might be more. These are the only ones I was able to get out of him, but he definitely has more as he's hidden more times than I can recall."

For someone who was so in love with Prometheus, it seemed strange that she was giving away all his secrets. She also didn't appear that distraught, which surprised me since she was sullen the other times he had left without her. Was there a clue in all this? Rather than be a lovesick puppy, she just looked uncharacteristically calm.

Mel must have noticed me staring at her, as she smiled a little. "You are wondering why I am calm, aren't you?"

My eyes widened, caught off guard, but I nodded my head.

She laughed. "It's easy. I can stay unflustered, thinking of all the things I am going to do to him when this is over. He will have wished he never stabbed me in the back like this."

"Get in line," Hades commented. "He kidnapped my daughter, and I call dibs on killing him."

Mel grinned. "I would like to see you beat me to him, god of the Underworld. I will take him into this realm to do some preliminary torture, and you can torture him all you want in the afterlife."

Hades seemed like he was taking that into consideration.

"What about the Underworld right now? Who is running it if both you and Persephone are here?" I asked. Chrys always mentioned that Hades rarely left due to his duties in the Underworld. I understand why this was more important to him, but I also didn't want to go to the Underworld and find it in pure chaos.

Hades answered, "Different gods that reside there are splitting up my duties for the time being. Hermes is also checking on it from time to time to make sure the dead are being delivered where they need to be. He owes me that much."

I felt there was a longer story there, but I decided not to pry further. There was still so much I didn't understand about this world, and I wasn't going to get my answers at that moment, nor did I need them.

I glanced over the list we had for gods that might help us and found it a lot shorter than the list of places to check. "Are we sure these are the only gods who we can contact? I feel we are missing some."

"This is the list of ones who owe me favors," Hades said. "There aren't many who would want to help us without me calling the favors that I have held on to for so long."

"What about Dionysius?" I asked. "He isn't on the list, but I don't see why he wouldn't help us."

"He didn't want to be involved the first time we went up to see him. What makes you think he would want to be on our side now?" Pothos asked.

I shrugged. "I guess I thought he'd know places Prometheus would have gone to. It seemed like they were close at one time, so perhaps he could help us find the hideout."

Pothos let out a sigh. "That is a possibility, as long as he is still where we left him months ago, though by the looks of him then, he probably wasn't going to go anywhere soon. It is worth a try, and I can take that journey with you."

Hades tapped his pen against the paper with the list of gods. "Persephone and I will cover the rest of the gods, as they'll likely only talk to us. As for you,

Mel…" He turned to her with a smirk. "You can stay here and torment AJ."

She smiled. "With pleasure."

CHAPTER 3

Chrys

"Take in slow, deep breaths, Vera. Inhale for one, two, three, four, five, and exhale for one, two, three, four, five," Circe said.

I was sitting cross-legged on a log in the middle of the forest that sat behind her house. I kept my eyes shut, feeling the small rays coming through the thick foliage. I could sense her circling me, likely monitoring my progress. However, it made me more nervous, and I couldn't concentrate.

Keeping a rhythmic breath, I did as she asked. We had been out there for what seemed like hours, but I had a feeling it probably was only ten minutes.

"You need to learn to calm your mind in order to

become stronger. You can't let your thoughts betray you if you are going to go up against Zeus."

That was easier said than done. I couldn't remember anything that had happened, so I didn't know what I should be thinking in the first place. Who was Zeus? Why was he trying to kill me? What was going on?

"Focus! I can tell your thoughts are filled with confusion."

I opened my eyes and looked at her. "I just woke up from some kind of fight with my memories gone. I think I am going to feel confused for quite some time. Why can't we focus on getting those memories back instead of becoming more powerful?"

Circe sighed as she stopped in front of me. "Because you are too powerful, and if something catches you off guard, I'm afraid you are going to lose all your senses and destroy everything around you."

Destroy everything around me? How was that possible? "You think I'm that powerful?"

"I know you are that powerful. If Zeus wanted you dead because of a threat, then that means you are potentially more powerful than him. We need to make sure that part of you is under control before it becomes unmanageable."

"I guess that makes sense. I just want to know my past is all. I have this overwhelming feeling that I lost a lot more than just my memories. Who was I before this?" I looked down at my dress. "Is this something I would really wear? Where am I from? There is so much I don't understand."

She grabbed my hand and squeezed it. "You are Papavera, daughter of Prometheus. You have the power over life and death, and if we don't get it under control, then you could destroy everything around you."

I didn't know if that made me feel better or worse. Life and death? How was that even possible?

"And that dress looks perfect on you, so of course it is something you would have loved. White suits you."

I wasn't sure if that really was true, as it seemed like I was wearing a costume. I wasn't sure why I felt that way, but in my heart, I could almost remember the person I used to be.

Shaking the feeling off, I closed my eyes again. "Okay, I'll give it a shot."

"Okay, breathe in for five seconds and out for five seconds."

I still wasn't sure how this breathing exercise would help me, but I did as she asked. Focusing on my breath, I let my mind go blank, only focusing on the counting and the energy that made up this island. It felt warming and relaxing, yet a cool breeze kept me alert to my surroundings. Birds sang in the background, pairing perfectly with the atmosphere. I wondered what the ocean water would feel like against my skin. I wanted more than anything to jump in later.

Shaking that thought away, I focused on my breath once again, matching it with the wilderness around me. I could feel the rhythm now, as everything seemed like a symphony. I could understand how all the pieces were coming together, and I tried to do the same for my own.

"That's it. Now I want you to focus on the tree you are sitting on."

I did as she asked. It was old, having fallen and died decades before. It had once been a huge magical tree that was home to many creatures. When it fell, many mourned it.

"Focus on its energy and life force. Do you feel the ember?"

I nodded. I did. It was small, as if the roots still held part of its soul.

"Bring it back. Make that force larger—large enough that the tree grows once more."

That was crazy. There was no way I could bring something this far gone back to life. That was against nature and everything that held the world together. I couldn't bring the deceased back.

Or could I?

My father and Circe had said that my powers were so great that Zeus wanted me dead. I supposedly had the power over life and death. Was that what they meant? Could I bring this tree back to life? Was that why Zeus was after me?

I focused on the energy that the stump still had. It was small, like heat from the coals in a fire. It was there, trying its best, but it only had a matter of time. I could sense it, but what could I do about it?

If it was like coals, then it needed more energy and more substance. Using my own energy, I focused on adding to it, as if I too had the energy of a tree. Life force was all the same. I didn't dare take away from anything around me for fear that my power to destroy would hurt anything else. No, I would use my own energy to bring life to this tree.

Working at it, keeping my focus on the tree's energy and nothing else, I began to add and form it to a great tree once again. The energy was there, now the physical would just have to follow suit.

That was something I had no idea how to begin. Sure I could give it energy, but how would the energy do anything to the physical realm? How would such a thing be possible?

As I tried to use my energy that was connected to will it back on the physical plane, I felt the stump begin to shake. My eyes shot open, and I quickly jumped off as the stump grew and grew up toward the sky, branches bushing out, growing larger with every passing second.

The tree climbed and climbed until it was the tallest standing object on all of the island. It towered over us, as grand as it once was. My mouth opened, not believing what I was seeing.

Did I do that? Was I really capable of this power?

Circe patted my back. "You did it. You brought this cedar back to the island. All of the creatures and plants that surround it will be in harmony with it once more. This is great progress."

That was only progress? What else did they think I could do?

"Let's head back. You deserve a huge dinner tonight. And Apollo should be back. You will be able to meet him—or I guess meet him again. You two used to know each other before your memories disappeared."

I nodded. "Yeah, that sounds good."

As I followed her back, something in my stomach said that it didn't want to talk to Apollo. But if my father trusted him to bring him into hiding with us, then why was my intuition telling me the opposite?

Dinner consisted of a vegetable pie mixed with a cheese sauce and covered with mashed potatoes and even more cheese. It was one of the best foods I had ever eaten, although I couldn't really remember the different foods I had before waking up, but my stomach insisted it was.

I chowed down on the meal, probably a little too quickly, and drank the herbal tea that Circe had made for me. She said it was full of herbs that would be helpful for regaining the energy I used but without keeping me up at night. I wasn't sure what was in it this time, but it tasted like roses and lavender, so I didn't complain. I couldn't imagine something with roses and lavender to be harmful to me, and I trusted Circe wouldn't try to hurt me. It didn't make sense that she would, as she was risking everything to hide me here in her domain. And it would have been easier to hurt me while I was unconscious for so long.

Across from me at the table sat Apollo. He had dirty-blond hair and a scruffy face. He wore a tank top and shorts, and I could tell he had a pendant under his shirt. I wasn't sure how I felt about him, as something inside me wanted to slap him, but nothing about the present warranted that reaction. Father sat next to me, also eating his meal quickly.

"Circe," my father began. "You really have outdone yourself with this meal. It is superb. Where was this in these past few days?"

Circe slapped him on the back of the head. "I was waiting for Vera to wake up before I made the good meals. Why would I waste my skills on the likes of you two?"

I chuckled and went back to finishing my meal. I probably was going to have seconds as this was very delicious.

"So, Vera." Apollo let my name linger a little, as if it

was amusing to him, calling me by that name. I wasn't sure why that was or why he would think anything about this was amusing. "Circe says you brought back an entire tree to life. How was that?"

I shrugged. "I don't know, it felt natural to me. I could feel the energy coming from the tree and just added to it to bring it back to what it was. The tree did the rest. It sprouted up and became the tree that it once was. I didn't really do much."

Father placed his hand on my back. "You did very well. That isn't something many gods can do. Even the ones that can would bring the tree back through a rebirth cycle, not to its full form like that. It is impressive."

I blushed. It didn't feel like I had done much, as it was my first day awake.

"Just wait for the days to come; you will be able to do anything and can take down Zeus," Apollo commented.

I shrugged. "I don't see what bringing a tree back to life would mean for defeating Zeus. I mean, I don't even see how he would have a problem with what I did."

"It is because he believes that everything has a certain life and death, and that shouldn't change. What you can do goes against that, not to mention it means you can bring on his death. He is more afraid of death than the rest of us," Prometheus explained. "He has been ruling for thousands of years, and he honestly needs to step down. Since he won't do that, it will be up to you to start a revolution."

Standing up, Prometheus smiled. "But don't worry, we are far from that. First we have to get you powerful enough and recall why you would want to do such a thing."

I nodded but wasn't sure if I believed in that. Was it really up to me to kill him? Why was this revolution so important to me?

What exactly had happened in my former life?

CHAPTER 4

Huntley

Pothos and I headed up toward Dublin where we believed Dionysius still resided. This time we drove in Pothos's red Mini Cooper, trying our best to get around all the huge puddles that were forming on the roads. Hydroplaning was never fun when you were in a hurry and not goofing off. What I really hated were the roundabouts that went the opposite way as opposed to America. It was very confusing, and it freaked me out. I kept leaning the incorrect way as he turned in to them.

There was a reason Pothos wouldn't let me drive.

Luckily there weren't many people on the road, as Pothos would have probably run them over. He drove fast, and I mean very fast. With the rain and the occasional sliding across a puddle, I felt like I was going to die. If it weren't for the fact Chrys might be in mortal danger, I would have yelled at him to slow down. But we needed to act quickly, and I could trust a god to be safe while driving unnatural speeds down a backcountry road.

At least that's what I kept telling myself as I kept a death grip on my seat.

Sliding across yet another puddle, I bit my tongue to suppress my scream. Was Pothos trying to get us killed? If we were killed, then we wouldn't be able to save Chrys.

"Maybe… just slow down a little?" I commented when I could finally breathe again.

Pothos shook his head. "We only have thirty minutes until the ferry closes and heads over to Dublin. If we miss that one, then we have to wait four hours."

"Ah. Then I guess step on it."

He did and went even faster than he had been going just minutes before. I screamed a little this time as we passed by some more fuzzy cows. They were adorable in general but looked very miserable in this rain, clearly gathered in a circle under the trees, trying to stay dry. It wasn't working—that was how heavy the rain was.

We didn't pass any cops on the way, which I was happy for. I wondered if Pothos could sense them or if we were just lucky. I wasn't going to say anything though, as I didn't want to jinx it. It felt like anytime we were about to make progress in the past year for helping Chrys, some weird curveball was thrown at us. Or we were betrayed. Or we were attacked...

I still couldn't believe Prometheus betrayed us like that. What was he even planning? What did he want to use Chrys for? When he was gone for so long, it must have been because he was making this backup plan. I should have trusted my gut and refused his help, but these gods were a lot more powerful than me, and it wasn't like I would have been able to save Chrys on my own.

I hated being a helpless human.

We made it to Holyhead, and Pothos slowed down to the appropriate speed so he wouldn't get pulled over. The ferry was just about finished loading up when we pulled our car on, and each of us let out a sigh.

"That was a close one. Now, better take any stomach medicine you might have. This is going to be a rather bumpy ride."

Pothos wasn't wrong. As we set off, the sea moved the boat a bit more than I would have liked. I tried my best not to vomit on the passenger that sat next to me as we looked out the glass window at the angry sea. This was probably the worst the waters could be before they would shut down the ferry.

I was just glad that they didn't.

"How long is this ferry ride?" I asked Pothos as I swallowed back some bile.

"Three hours." He sighed. "So go find some stomach meds, if there are any left."

I nodded and headed toward the little convenience area. Luckily there were a couple of packs left, and I bought one and split it with an elderly lady and her husband. It wasn't like I needed the whole pack of ginger chews anyway, and they appeared quite miserable.

Taking a seat next to Pothos, I leaned back and stared up at the ceiling. This, actually, made my seasickness even worse. I moved my head so I could see the ocean again. "So, what should we do now?"

"Ride this boat, I suppose."

"Right, but what should we do to kill the time and not think about this storm?"

Pothos laughed. "We chill. There isn't anything we can do unless you want to play some traveling game or something."

I glanced around. "I spy… something… purple."

Pothos nodded at the woman across the way. "That woman's matching bra and underwear."

My face turned red. "How would I know what color her bra and underwear are?"

Pothos grinned. "You might not, but I do. And damn she's hot."

I rolled my eyes. Maybe just keeping to myself would be for the best.

The three-hour ride was long and tedious, but I was glad to be back on land when it was all over. I did not look forward to doing that again on the way back.

"We have three hours to go talk to Dionysius and be able to take a ferry back tonight. Otherwise, we will have to wait until morning, unless you want to take the two a.m. ferry."

I gave him a look. "Who the hell would want to go on a ferry ride at two a.m.?"

He shrugged. "Night shift workers probably. Anyway, help me find a spot to park near that bar."

The bar appeared just as it did last time we were there. It had felt like so long ago, and I wondered if he really would still be there right where we had found him the first time.

The window wipers swept across the window as fast as they could, but they couldn't completely clear the rain fast enough to be able to see out well. Luckily I was able to find a spot on the side of the street a couple of blocks away, and Pothos quickly parked.

"That was probably one of the best spots I have found in a city in a long time. Now let's get a move on it."

We unbuckled our seat belts and made a run for it,

trying not to get soaked as the rain seemed to be coming down even harder.

"You would think Zeus would let up by now!" I yelled over the thunder.

Pothos laughed. "What do you expect from a god who throws tantrums and holds grudges? The storm will hopefully die off in a few weeks, if we are lucky."

I hoped it wouldn't be that long, as Chrys was in trouble that very minute. There wasn't time to spare.

We entered the bar to find only a few customers scattered across the area. I glanced around but didn't see that red-headed alcoholic anywhere.

"He's not here," I said in defeat.

Pothos held up a finger. "One second." He went up to the bartender, a tall man with a thick mustache. "Is that drunk ginger fellow still living upstairs?"

He nodded. "Yeah, but he just gave me notice and said he was leaving tonight."

Pothos smiled. "Thanks." Then he turned and nodded to me. "Upstairs, quick. He's going to make a run for it."

We hurried up the stairs and found the door ajar. Pushing it open, we found Dionysius swiftly packing a duffel bag. Glancing up, he saw us.

"Shit."

Pothos nodded. "Yeah, shit. You didn't pack fast enough." He closed the door behind us. "Now talk.

Where is Prometheus hiding?"

Dionysius shrugged. "I have no idea. We aren't as close as you think we are."

"Then why were you running?" I asked.

"Because everyone thinks we are." He pointed at the ceiling. "And because another god is freaking out right now. None of us are safe. He is going to start coming after each and every one of us, trying to see if we know something. We know nothing!"

"But you do know some of his favorite places to hang out. Start listing them out." Pothos took a seat across from Dionysius.

Dionysius sighed as he collapsed on the bed. "I don't know. It's been a long time."

"Well, start remembering."

"What's the point? Hell, I don't even know what this is completely about. What did Prometheus even do this time?"

"He kidnapped Chrys, forced her to drink the water of Lethe, and is teaching her to use her powers so she can kill Zeus," Pothos explained. "Now spill."

Dionysius glanced at both of us. "I don't see what the problem is. Don't we want her to take down Zeus?"

"He could be hurting Chrys," I explained. "And if Zeus finds her first, he might kill her right then and there. I won't allow that—not after everything."

"Look," Dionysius explained. "I don't know if you

have noticed, but I am scared of Zeus. I don't want to know if he finds her. I don't care what Prometheus did. I don't care if she survives or not. All I care about is saving my own skin. And I don't see how helping you two will do that."

Before I could start cussing him out, Pothos interjected. "She is the daughter of Hades. Yes, if you help us, Zeus might come after you. Or he might come after you just because he thinks you helped us. You know Zeus—he doesn't think rationally.

"But do you want to be on the bad side of Hades? If you die, you have to face him, and if he finds out you were holding back information that could have saved his precious daughter, he will torture you for an eternity in the heart of Tartarus."

Dionysius audibly gulped.

"Do you want to piss off Hades, or do you want to help Hades? I mean, either way, Zeus might come after you. Or you could come with us and we will do our best to keep you safe. Hell, I have a bunch of connections in London. I could easily keep you hidden there. Zeus is a bit preoccupied at the moment, so you will go unnoticed."

Dionysius pondered on his options for a bit. "You promise you will bring me to London safe and sound if I tell you some of his hideouts? Even if they aren't the place he is hiding right now?"

Pothos nodded. "I pinky swear. You won't have to do anything else to help us either. You can go get drunk in some corner of a bar for the rest of eternity for all I care. Just help us out this once."

Dionysius was silent for a moment, then nodded. "Fine. I'll give you a list of the places I know. I have a feeling though, knowing how crafty Prometheus is, he probably isn't somewhere anyone would ever think of."

"We have to keep trying though," I said. "And maybe someone at one of the hideouts knows where he is."

Pothos nodded. "Yeah. We aren't leaving any stone unturned at this point."

Dionysius grabbed a piece of paper and wrote down the places. Pothos pulled out his phone and took a picture and texted it to Mel to add to the list. I glimpsed at the list. There were seven places on it, three of which we already knew of.

So we added four more places to look. Great.

"What about Apollo?" I asked. "Do you know anywhere he would hide?"

Dionysius raised an eyebrow. "Apollo? He's helping Prometheus?"

Pothos and I nodded.

"Huh. I wouldn't have thought those two would work together. Well, knowing Apollo, it will have to be somewhere warm and nice. That could help narrow it down for you."

"Yeah, but that could also be something they think we would figure out and hide in the opposite location," I added. "And even if he's in the sun, that doesn't narrow it down either."

Dionysius shrugged. "Well, it is no longer my problem." He grabbed his duffel bag and smiled. "You promised me a hiding spot, Pothos. Now lead the way."

CHAPTER 5

Chrys

I still didn't feel comfortable about any of this.

The next couple of days came and went, and Circe taught me more on how to feel the energy inside a dying thing and how to bring it back to life. We worked only with plants to start with, whose death is long and drawn out as it slowly becomes one with the earth. There was a lot of vitality in plants, as they never truly died but gave birth to new life so generously. I liked that I could feel the rebirth cycle in them.

I wasn't sure what it was, but it still felt like a crime bringing these plants back to life, as if I had brought them eternal torture. They were meant to die to bring nutrients, but as I restored their lifeforce, it was like I was taking away from what they really wanted. I could feel it in their energy—an anger and resentment for being alive once again instead of passing off their life to another.

I didn't tell Circe that, however, as I felt she would think I was making up excuses. But it was a fact—I could feel the energy cry out to me. Was this my power? Was I supposed to be able to see this?

It made sense though, as I was supposed to have control over life and death. The more we worked on it, the more I understood why Zeus would have wanted me dead. No one should be able to mess with nature like this.

I kept my mouth shut though and did what was asked of me. Circe and my father knew more about what was going on than I did. I couldn't remember anything—I didn't even understand how the worlds came into existence. Perhaps there was a reason I was like this— perhaps it was indeed something I needed to do.

Today Circe brought me out into the middle of the woods, just as she did on most days, except today she carried a bow and some arrows in a quiver. It made me worried what she was going to do with them and if it had to do with our training.

The weather was nice, like it had been most previous days. The air was warm but not too warm with a cool breeze that softened the impact of the sun. If it was up to me, I would spend every moment out there and just relax in the sun instead of train. If we were hidden so well, why couldn't we just chill there for an eternity? It was paradise, and I couldn't see how anything else in this world could be better.

"Circe, how long have you lived here?" I questioned as we walked even farther.

She looked up at the sky. "Oh, I don't know. I guess it's been at least three thousand years now. Time flies when you are a god."

"Three thousand years? That is a long time. And no one knows of this island."

"Humans tried to come to it once, but no one has come upon it since then."

"Then why do we have to train? Why can't we just stay here? If it is nice enough for you to stay so long, why can't we?"

Circe's eyes widened as if taken by surprise, but then she simply smiled. "Because no one cared I had disappeared. But after your incident with Zeus, he will be searching high and low, and it is only a matter of time until he finds us here."

I guess she had a point since apparently there were people after me. Zeus wanted me dead, and I didn't know how many other people were looking for me. I hated not knowing the full scale of what was going on or what had actually happened. If only I could remember everything.

Before I could feel bad for myself even more, we stopped near a tree trunk, and Circe pointed farther into the forest.

"Do you see that deer?" she whispered.

There was a small doe in the distance that was grazing the grass that covered the forest floor. I nodded, a little worried. "Yes."

Pulling out an arrow, she shot the deer right then and there. I gasped and ran to it. I couldn't believe she would do something like that to such a harmless creature.

"Heal him," Circe said as she walked over to me. She pulled the arrow out of the deer's stomach. "Heal him before he dies."

I couldn't believe what I was hearing. She did this just to test me. My heart raced, feeling as if I would be unable to perform such a task. It was one thing when it was plants whose energy was like a coal. This creature's life force was like a burning flame, and it was going to go out soon as it wildly flared.

Knowing it was the only way to save it, I closed my eyes and focused on its life force. It was there for sure, but I had very little time to do anything. I took in a deep breath and put in everything I could to help the poor creature.

As I closed my eyes, I listened to the energy. It was

confused, not sure why its life was suddenly ending. Tears fell down my cheeks as I felt responsible for what had happened. I couldn't let this creature suffer anymore.

I heard the creature shuffle and opened my eyes to watch it frantically get up and dash away farther into the woods. I had done it—I had saved it.

Circe patted me on the back. "You did well, Vera. I didn't expect you to make such progress this fast. You really are attuned to your powers. I am very proud of you."

I smiled a little but still disturbed about everything that had happened. "I just don't understand how this is going to take down Zeus."

"In due time, my dear child. There is a lot more you can do with this power. We are just beginning to grasp what you are capable of. I doubt it will be long, however, until you master your power of life and death."

And death. They all kept saying that, but I didn't quite understand what they meant. I understood how I had the power over life, as I had been bringing things back to life, but death? How did that differ from just simply killing things, just like Circe almost did to the deer? Was there something more to it than that?

She gave me another pat. "I am going to head back and start supper. If you want, you can stay here for a while. I trust you know your way back to my cottage?"

I nodded. "Yeah, I do. And I think I will stay out here for a bit. I like the forest and want some time to think."

"All right. I will head back and let Prometheus know you are fine. The moment he sees me come back without you, he is going to freak. He worries about you, especially after how Zeus almost killed you. You have a very strong and thoughtful father."

"Yeah," I said. "I suppose I do."

With that, she left me sitting there. I took in a deep breath and let the surrounding forest take me in. It felt like it had been so long since I was truly alone. I never felt alone in my room as I knew there was always someone outside the door. But out here, it felt like I was truly by myself and free to think my own thoughts.

I closed my eyes and listened to the birds in the distance. They sang their songs out to the world, not caring about anything else. I wanted to be as free as them—able to spread my wings instead of staying in this cage that was this island. Don't get me wrong, it was a rather large island, but I still felt trapped. What else was out there? What was I missing? Who was I missing?

A knot formed in my chest. I felt like there was someone out there I should be thinking about, but I had no idea who that person was. They must have been special if I was still able to feel their energy even with my memories gone like this.

I placed my hand on my heart and tried to remember. If I could control energy enough to bring something back to life, then perhaps I could bring my memories back in the same way. I took in a deep breath and let it out slowly, just as Circe had taught me.

Focusing on the feeling that was coming from my heart, I tried to open it up so I could remember. It felt as if something dark and aqueous was surrounding it, engulfing it so that I couldn't do anything to get to it. I tried harder and harder to clear the substance, but every time I dug further, my head started to pound harder and harder.

My eyes shot open and I gasped. My head was throbbing as if someone had stabbed hundreds of needles into my skull. Why did that happen? Why couldn't I remember?

I got up and made my way back to the cottage. Although I didn't want to tell Circe I had a headache because I was trying to remember, I did want her to give me something to help with the pain. It was unbearable.

As I returned to the beach, I saw the beautiful ocean glistening in the setting sun. It was gorgeous, and I realized I hadn't gone in to test the water yet, as I was kept busy with Circe's lessons. I grabbed my aching head. I guess I would wait until I felt a little bit better before jumping in.

A delicate song surrounded me. It wasn't like a voice but almost a hypnotic sound. Whatever it was swept away any pain I was having, and I finally felt free.

The song continued, lingering in my mind, causing an almost euphoric feeling. I wanted to hear it forever. It felt like it was carrying me, and before I knew it, I was only a couple of feet away from the water.

"Don't!" I felt someone grab me and pull me back.

I snapped out of whatever trance I was in and turned to find my father standing there, his hand around my wrist. His face was pale and his eyes were filled with worry.

"Don't go into the water," he repeated.

"What?" I asked.

"Don't go into the water. There are monsters lurking in those waters, and they will take you to Zeus."

I glanced out at the water. It made sense that Zeus would have sent things from all over to look for me. But would they really be able to notice if I simply stepped in?

"I'll stay away. I'm sorry I almost—"

He scratched his head. "No, it's my fault. I should have told you earlier. I meant to, but I just…" He scratched the back of his head, appearing worried. "A lot is going on, and I don't know how to handle it all. I'm sorry."

I shook my head. "No, you have no reason to be sorry. You have kept me safe all this time, and I appreciate it. I'm doing what I can to be powerful enough on my own. Then you won't have to worry as much about me."

Father smiled and gestured toward the cottage. "Should we go inside? I have a feeling Circe will be mad if we let her food get cold."

I nodded and laughed. "Yeah, I think you might be right."

CHAPTER 6

Huntley

The storm was still not letting up, which made traveling around London even worse than normal. I hated walking around in this kind of rain, as the wind made holding an umbrella impossible. Luckily all we needed to do was deliver Dionysius to the hideout Pothos promised, and then we could head back to the flat where Mel awaited us. Hopefully she hadn't completely destroyed AJ yet as I wanted a chance to take out my frustrations on him.

I was glad Dionysius was able to give us the names of a couple of new locations, but I had a feeling he was right about Prometheus probably hiding somewhere he had never gone before, or at least not in a very long time. He knew we would be looking for him and asking around, so he would have had to go somewhere no one would guess or have linked him to.

But it would have to be somewhere his plan would work.

One never realized how big the world really was until you had to look for someone. All the times I tried to run away from my home in Philadelphia, I was caught though. I guess I was never smart enough to actually hide. Perhaps I wanted to be found and saved in the end.

But there hadn't been anyone to save me back then.

Then I died and Chrys found me and brought more meaning to my life or death or soul or whatever. So I would stop at nothing to find her and save her.

We opened the door to find AJ strapped to a spinning wheel against the wall, knives sticking out of him. Mel smiled as she saw us and threw the last knife she had in her hand. It hit the wheel, inches away from AJ's face.

"Damn, I missed."

Tears and blood were streaming down AJ's face. "Why did you leave me with this psychotic bitch?"

I glanced over at Mel again, who was wearing a black circus-like outfit. She was really into this act. I couldn't blame her but also made a note to never, ever piss her off.

"Can I have a round?" I asked, having always wanted

to throw knives at the fair but never having enough money to.

Nodding, she skipped over to AJ and pulled out the knives that littered his body and the board. He screamed as more blood soaked his clothes. I glanced over to Pothos, who didn't seem as worried about whether the neighbors would hear the screaming.

Pothos saw my face. "Don't worry, Mel spelled this flat ages ago so no one could hear anything going on. Mostly because of the shit Prometheus and she did in this room."

I thought about responding but then decided not to. I shook my head. I really didn't want to know. Turning to Mel, she gave me her knives.

"Have at it."

I grinned, finding this to be the best way to wait for Hades and Persephone. I hadn't played such a fun game in a long time. I missed going to carnivals and knew that once I found Chrys and we were safe, I would have to take her to a carnival that had games like this.

Or perhaps we could still torture AJ instead and center all the games around his torture.

Setting all but one knife down, I chucked the first knife at AJ. It didn't stick but did slice him straight in the calf, as the edges were very sharp.

"Fuck you, you stupid human!" AJ shouted.

Mel shook her head. "No, no, you have it all wrong.

You need to hold the knife like a hammer." She showed me with her own knife. "Then make sure you are about three meters from the target so the knife can make a full rotation, and when you throw, keep your wrist strong and don't change it."

I nodded slowly, trying to remember everything she said. It sounded straightforward. Who knew there was so much that went into knife throwing. I gripped my knife, holding it like a hammer, then threw it at the target. I could see AJ's worry as I let go of the knife. It hit the board right next to his face. AJ let out a slight cry.

"Great, now hit the target." Pothos laughed as he took a seat on the couch. He simply watched us as we played our games.

I gave him a look, then tried again. I focused on the wheel spinning and knew I should aim for his torso, as it was the biggest area. I threw the knife, and it hit him straight in the arm. I guess I still wasn't that great at aiming, but at least I hit something.

"I did it!"

"Fuck you!" AJ screamed. "Fuck you all! When I get out of here, I'm going straight to my father and telling him what you did to me!"

Pothos laughed. "What are you, a Malfoy?"

"What's a Malfoy?" he asked as he kept spinning. I was starting to get dizzy just watching him.

Pothos shook his head. I laughed a little, understanding the reference. Even I read Harry Potter as a child.

It also didn't matter if AJ got away and told his father what we did as I doubted he even cared about AJ. Poseidon was only using him to get knowledge about Chrys, and none of us had knowledge about her. He would just brush AJ aside and keep looking for her. From my understanding, there were a lot of demigods out there, both on Earth and in the Underworld.

Almost as if the gods couldn't keep it in their pants.

"I want to give this a try." Pothos got up and grabbed a knife. Taking aim, he threw it straight into AJ's hand. I was surprised that AJ was still awake with all the pain and that his body didn't go into shock, not to mention just dizzy from slowly spinning around and around. I guess it really did suck to be immortal.

AJ's little plan backfired. He should have just stayed in the Underworld where he could have lived in paradise for eternity. Instead, he was in this mess and there was no way any of us were going to let him go.

I grabbed a knife and threw it at the board. I missed again.

"God damn it!" I yelled.

"What am I damning?" a voice said behind us. I turned to find Hades and Persephone standing there. Hades' eyes moved to the makeshift spinning knife target. Lifting his hand, a knife went flying into it, and he then threw the knife straight into AJ's eye. AJ screamed even louder than before.

"Whoa, nice shot!" I commented.

"Thanks. Now, please tell me you received some information from Dionysius."

Pothos answered. "Yes, we got a list of some more places, and some overlapped with the ones we already knew. I promised Dionysius that you would be nice to him in the Underworld for helping us. I hid him in one of the spots where my brothers are. They should be quiet for a while."

Hades nodded. "Good. That's at least some positive news for us."

I didn't like how he said that. "Why, what happened?"

"Everyone we know is a selfish asshole," Persephone said as she kicked off her black heels. "None of them wanted to go against Zeus at this time and refused to help."

My eyes widened. "None of them?"

Hades sighed as he straightened his suit jacket. "None that would be of help for us. Of course, some in the Underworld would assist, but they are busy as it is. Luckily it doesn't seem there are many that are on Zeus's side either, so it's not like we are completely outnumbered. They just want to stay neutral. It is, however, just the five of us."

"And my sirens," Persephone added. "Luckily they can turn into both fishlike sirens and birdlike sirens, which means they are scanning everything. They are being extra careful not to be spotted by Poseidon or Zeus though and are calling out a song that only she can hear. But so far, they haven't found anything."

The sirens could also turn into mermaids? Now that I wanted to see. I shook my head, ignoring those thoughts. I saw Pothos smirk as if he had been reading my mind. I stuck my tongue out at him, then turned back to the board.

Five of us. To look over twenty-three different places. This wasn't going to be easy.

"We can group them into separate regions. Then there are really only seven areas we need to check." Mel went to the board and color-coded the areas. "I still think it will be somewhere sunny, but if he is expecting us to deduce that, then we have no choice but to check them all."

Hades went on. "If we are going to split up, I still think Huntley should go with Pothos. No offense, Huntley, but you are human, and if any god or creature finds you snooping around those areas, they might kill you."

"That's fair," I said. "I'll stay with Pothos. But what about AJ?"

Mel's eyes shone. "Don't worry, I can take him with me. I always love having a pack mule."

AJ whimpered a little as the wheel kept spinning. I would have felt sorry for him, but he definitely deserved it.

Persephone put her hands on her hips. "Then Hades and I can split up. The question is, who is taking which area?"

"Huntley, you are from the States, right? Maybe the two of us should check those areas." Pothos tapped his finger on the different locations in the US.

"I don't know if that would be a good idea," I began. "I mean, I might kind of know some areas, but I died over there, and I don't know if someone might recognize me. It's a big country, but knowing my luck…"

"He has a point. Why don't the two of you go to Japan and China, and I will take the US. Persephone can search the Caribbean, and Mel can go to the Mediterranean. Then after we check those areas, Pothos and Huntley can scour Russia, Mel can look in the North Sea, I will search Australia, and Persephone can head back here and make sure Prometheus isn't right under our noses."

We all nodded. Although it was a mission to find Chrys, I was sort of excited to head to Japan. It wasn't somewhere I had ever dreamed I would be able to go, yet here I was, flying to a bunch of countries in as short a time as possible.

Pothos turned to me. "Well, should we get packed?"

I nodded. "Yeah. When will the plane be leaving? How much should I pack?"

Pothos laughed. "Oh, we won't be taking the plane. We don't have time for that, not to mention the storms make flying less fun. We will be using a shortcut."

I gave Pothos a look as we climbed up the stairs. "If we could use shortcuts, why didn't we do that to find Dionysius?"

"Because we didn't want Zeus to find out about Dionysius. Right now it's more of a battle of time, and Zeus might have these locations already. We want to get there first even if it alerts him. We will be given that little extra time."

I guess that made sense, but it still made me roll my eyes. "Whatever. As long as it doesn't make me throw up, I don't care."

"It might. I can't promise anything."

I threw a punch at him as he stepped into his room and closed the door, causing my knuckles to hit the wood instead. I cursed as I entered my own room and quickly gathered my things.

I wouldn't be long now. I would save Chrys even if it was the last thing I did.

CHAPTER 7

Chrys

I couldn't sleep.

I lay there, tossing and turning in my bed. There was too much on my mind these past few days that it was lucky that I'd gotten any sleep at all. I wondered if gods really needed to sleep in the first place. It seemed that the rest of them just rested rather than slumbered.

But that didn't change the fact I was lying there wide-awake.

The smell of the salty air wafting into the room made me glance over at the open window that let the moonlight pour into my bedroom. The moon glistened beautifully in the sky, outshining the stars. The stars scattered throughout the night sky reminded me of something. It was similar to the blue shimmering sky that never changed. What was it?

My head started to pound. This was unbearable—every time I began to remember something, my head started to hurt. Was there something trying to stop me from remembering? And if so, what was it? Who caused this?

Was it Zeus?

I couldn't even imagine what Zeus looked like. I knew he was the god of all gods, but that was about it. Why did he hate me so much? Were there other gods with him who wanted me dead? Were there other gods on my side besides the three in this household? Where were they?

I tried to imagine what the rest of the world looked like. I understood that there was a world out there with different places and people, but I couldn't imagine any of it. Was it all water? Was there more land? What did other people look like? Was it just gods, or were there other types of people?

Remembering nothing was beyond frustrating.

At least I could talk. I still could converse and understood how to communicate, what food was, animals, and all that. The parts that were missing in my mind had to do with people and locations.

Which made me wonder why.

Sighing, I sat up and debated what to do. I didn't like

lying there, letting my thoughts take me somewhere I didn't want to go. I needed a distraction or maybe some food. Yeah, a snack sounded good, and I was sure there was leftover fruit in the fridge. Eating a few wouldn't hurt.

Getting up, I headed toward the kitchen, creeping along as quietly as I could. I didn't want to wake anyone and let them know I was snooping around even though all I wanted was a snack. There wasn't anything wrong with getting food, but I felt like I was committing a sin by wandering around at night.

Although they said they were on my side, I couldn't help noticing that they always seemed to have an eye on me, as if looking for something wrong. They constantly looked worried and concerned. It was creepy and I hated it. Why wouldn't they tell me what was on their mind? Why couldn't they do something to get my memories back?

And what was up with the ocean?

It made me really sad that I couldn't go into the water. It looked so nice and refreshing—I wanted to feel its softness engulf me as I dunked my head under. Oh well, I guess if there were creatures on the lookout for me, it would be safer to simply stay away.

That is, if Father wasn't lying to me.

He had no reason to lie, I supposed. What would he have to gain by helping me? He was risking his life with all this. At least that's what it seemed like. But then again, I didn't remember anything before waking up here.

Opening the fridge, I grabbed a handful of strawberries. That would do for the time being. I popped one in my mouth and sat on the couch in the living room. The window opened out to the ocean, and I stared out at it.

Even from this far away, I could still hear the song I heard hours before. It was soft and melodious. I wondered if anyone else could hear it or if it was just me. I let it soothe me as I ate more of the strawberries.

It was calming and almost familiar, as if it had the answers to everything and I could simply walk toward it, let it consume me, and all my worries would be gone. I wanted to know what kind of creature could make such a sound, as I imagined them to be something very beautiful. Could something evil make that sound? Was it really Zeus who sent them to me, or did it have to do with something else?

Before I knew it, I had forgotten about everything else except the song. It was calling to me—it wanted me to come back to the water.

Standing up, I took the few steps to the front door and placed my hand on the knob. I was just about to open it when I heard a loud thud.

I blinked, coming back to where I was. What was I

doing? I shook my head and turned to where I heard another thud. It was coming from Father's room.

Creeping over, I listened to it again. Instead of the noise, I heard voices.

"Damn Prometheus, and people thought I was rough." It was Apollo.

I backed away. Nope, I did not want to hear that. It was wrong—oh so wrong. I swallowed back some bile and started to turn toward my door.

"Shh, Chrys might hear you," Prometheus said. I kept back more bile. Nothing was worse than hearing your parents doing something you didn't want to think about.

Apollo's voice chimed in. "You mean Vera?"

I stopped and turned. Why did my supposed father call me a different name? What was going on? I let the name linger in my mind. Chrys…

Pain shot through my head, making me want to listen more—in case more secrets would be revealed.

"You knew what I meant."

Apollo responded. "Yeah, but you are the one who should be careful. You don't want her to remember her past, and hearing that name might trigger something."

Sneaking back to the door, I listened further. What did he mean they didn't want me to remember? What the hell was going on?

Prometheus whispered, "There is no way she will regain her memories. The power of Lethe will keep her from recalling anything."

"Just be careful," Apollo began. "You risked everything for this. And somehow talked me into helping your sorry ass."

"Hey, I thought you liked my ass."

"You know what I meant. I've had to stay indoors anytime the moon was out. You know what that's like for a wolf like me?" Apollo whined.

"Your sister will spot you right away if you stick your head outside for even just a second. She is obsessed with you. It's kind of creepy."

"Yeah, I know. But you've got to love her for that. She's dedicated."

"She's a stalker."

"Oh, and Mel isn't? She's going to kill you the moment she finds you, you know that, right?"

"Well, by then I will have defeated Zeus and become ruler of Olympus. She will have to obey me, along with everyone else."

"Should I call you my king then?"

I heard Prometheus laugh. "You can call me whatever you like."

There were more noises—ones I didn't want to think about and decided I had heard enough of the other stuff. I scurried back to my room. I quickly shut the door behind me and leaned my back against it.

What was that? Why did they not tell me their real

names? Why didn't they want me to remember anything? What the hell was going on?

Apollo had mentioned something about being a wolf. That triggered a memory of a wolf standing in front of me. Was that him? When did we meet before? What was the circumstance? There were too many thoughts swirling through my head. I needed to go outside and take a breath.

There was a problem, however. I didn't want to go out the front door, afraid that someone might hear me. Now that I knew Apollo and my father, or whoever he was to me, were awake, I didn't want to go through the hallway again. So instead, I climbed up to my window and got out of the house that way.

Something about sneaking out seemed familiar, but I tried not to think about it. I didn't want another headache. And the names they mentioned. Mel and Artemis, they seemed familiar as well.

Instead of going toward the water, I decided to head into the woods. I still wasn't sure what it was I was hearing coming from the ocean, but I didn't want to deal with it just that moment. I already had a lot on my plate.

I went deeper and deeper into the woods until I couldn't spot the cottage or the ocean any longer. I sat down on the dirt and let tears flow from my eyes.

There was no one to trust—I had nothing. I had no

way to get out of there, not knowing if what Prometheus had said was true about the creatures looking for me to report to Zeus, and I didn't know if they were really who they said they were. Was Zeus really wanting to kill me, or was that just a lie? Was it a risk I was really going to take?

So much confusion was running through my head that I started to feel something inside me begin to spark out. It was black and felt like raw energy. Opening my eyes, I found that the large bush that was in front of me was dead.

What in the world? Did I do that? I shut my eyes again. No, that couldn't be happening. That was crazy.

I just wanted to go home, wherever that might be. I just wanted to know who I really was and what was really going on.

More energy released from me, and it felt as if it had gone every which way. The energy became stronger and stronger, and it slowly consumed me.

Whatever it was, I didn't want it to take control of me. I was the one who was in control.

Pushing it back, I slowly opened my eyes. Not only was the bush dead but so were the five trees and foliage all surrounding me. It was like a circle of death radiating from me.

What was happening? Was it me? Was this what they meant when they said I had the power of death?

I closed my eyes and reached out to the plant's life force. It was gone—there was nothing left. No, no I couldn't do something like this. It wasn't natural.

I tried to grab at whatever energy I could to reverse it. I had to do something. It wasn't these plants' fault that I was angry.

Something clicked and the life force came back, but it was very faint. I worked at it, pushing at the energy to be replenished. Finally I felt it restore and opened my eyes to find the plants were back to normal. I let out a deep breath.

So this was my power. Maybe they hadn't been lying —I was strong and Zeus really did want me dead.

But then what was Prometheus' part in all this? And even though he lied, could I trust that he was on my side?

CHAPTER 8

Huntley

Using the god's passage was not the funnest thing in the world. In fact, it made me pretty sick. It was probably the second worst journey I had been on, the first being when we escaped the Underworld.

I tried not to hurl all over Pothos, as I didn't think he would appreciate that. He would probably have left me in the middle of Japan and continued the journey without me. Gesturing toward the forest, Pothos let me vomit behind a tree. Luckily it didn't seem like anyone noticed, as Pothos kept a lookout.

Once my stomach settled, I glanced around. Holy shit, I was in Japan. Although I knew it was going to happen, it was all so surreal. We stood in front of a shrine. It was night time, which I was glad for, as otherwise I expected a lot of people to be walking around.

The shrine was huge, with a giant rope thicker than my body, which I didn't think was possible. How did they twist all that fiber together? It must have been heavy. It looked cool though.

"Where exactly in Japan are we?" I asked Pothos as he started to move around the shrine.

"Izumo. It is where the gods of Japan were said to reside during the month of October. This place was very spiritual during that time with lots of festivals."

It was actually almost October. "Wait, so are the Japanese gods real?"

"It's complicated. Mostly, all the gods people worshipped around the world are just us with different names."

That… kind of made sense. A lot of gods were similar in what they did. I guess I never looked at it that way.

"But if all the gods will be coming in October, why would he hide here?"

Pothos shrugged. "I don't think he is here, but someone might know where he is since he liked to come here often and party. And man, is this place a party in October. It's been a few decades, but I still feel hungover from whatever they were serving."

We hurried into the woods behind the shrine. I gasped at what we found: a giant bonfire with a ton of people dancing around it. How did no human come across this? Was it hidden from their view like what Pothos did with his flat so no one heard screaming? I decided not to ask. I was past the point of asking about those things.

"Pothos! Come join us!"

So it was people that Pothos knew. He seemed a little on edge when we approached; this must have been why.

"I can't, you guys. I have to find Prometheus."

Three of the gods ran over. They wore what I would describe as hippie clothes. Not the old seventies hippies but more of the modern spiritual loose clothing. They even wore little flower crowns. All of them looked similar to Pothos, and I wondered if they were somehow related, although it seemed as if all the gods were related one way or another.

The taller god grabbed Pothos' hands. "It has been too long, brother. Please join us!"

The other two nodded.

Brother? So those were his siblings. Or it was one of those cult-type families. I still wasn't sure.

The one who looked closest to Pothos added, "You used to join us all the time. We have a duty to fulfill the wishes of all who come here, and you know as well as I that most of the wishes have to do with love."

Pothos sighed. "How about I promise I will come here after I find Prometheus? So if you help us find him, I will join you."

All their eyes lit up.

The brother who held his hands smiled. "You promise?"

Pothos nodded. "I do."

He let go of Pothos' hand and clapped his hands together. "Well then, let me tell you what our father's brothers' nephew's cousin's former roommate said!"

I tried to follow what relationship that was, but I got lost. I supposed it didn't really matter.

Pothos sighed. "What did he say?"

"He said he saw Prometheus a few months ago, snooping around some islands, as if looking for one in particular."

So we were right—it was an island. But that didn't narrow it down at all.

"So where is Aether now?" Pothos asked.

Wait, so he knew who they meant with that relationship list? Why didn't this guy just say his name? I kept my mouth shut, knowing Pothos would smack me if I made any sarcastic remarks. Besides, I might offend them and they wouldn't tell us where we needed to go.

"He is in Hong Kong, in the Mong Kok district. I can give you the address."

"Please do. We have little time."

The tall man hurried over to write down the address on whatever scrap paper he had with him. The other two waited with us.

The man who appeared similar to Pothos looked me over up and down a couple of times and leaned on the other's shoulder. "So, brother, who is this?"

"This is Huntley. He is a human. Huntley, these are my brothers Anteros and Himeros." Anteros was the one who looked most like him, and Himeros was the one with a shaggy beard. "The one over there is Eros."

"Nice to meet you," I said. I really didn't care one way or the other but wanted to get out of there. It was rather weird seeing so many of the same face.

"Pothos, I heard that Hades had a daughter and that is what you are after. Is that true?" Anteros asked.

He nodded. "Yeah. She is the most powerful goddess I have ever met. She could take down Olympus if she wanted. That is why we have to save her from Prometheus."

"And Apollo?" Himeros asked. "Isn't he with them as well?"

"Yeah, he is."

"I never thought Apollo would stoop so low as to help Prometheus. He must be very bored," Anteros commented.

Himeros agreed, nodding. "Yeah, but he is a wild

one. He will also have to stay inside during the night, or his sister will see him."

Pothos snapped his finger. "Artemis. I never thought about that. She would be a great help."

Eros stepped back up and handed Pothos the paper. "Too bad she doesn't listen to anyone. I doubt you could get her on your side, especially since she probably blames all of you for why her brother is gone."

Pothos sighed. "That's true. She has a strange fixation on him. But it is a thought…" He looked down at the paper. "Thank you, brothers, you have been a great help. Also, Zeus will probably be coming here soon, so make sure to stay inside when he does. He has been rage storming again."

"We will, and we won't tell him what we told you. It wouldn't be as fun and also because we don't want to see you die. Now get out of here so you can find Prometheus and then join us!"

I knelt down in the alleyway, vomiting.

The second time was even worse than the first. I thought for sure that it would be a bit easier, but I was terribly wrong. The bile that splattered the ground agreed. I doubted I had anything left in my stomach.

"I guess humans aren't meant for the god passage. Sorry about that," Pothos said as he leaned against the wall, watching me unload my already-empty stomach.

I spat out the rest of the spit that was still in my mouth and wiped my face. "Yeah, you don't have to tell me twice."

"At least you only need to do it one more time." Pothos smiled.

"I thought we were going to Russia next?"

Pothos shrugged. "That depends on what Aether has to say. It seems he ran into Prometheus a while back when he was looking for some island. That means Aether knows what island he's on or at least which one he was looking for. He must have been doing all that when he said he was looking for Dionysius."

I knew he was up to something back then. I should have trusted my gut instead of just blindly trusting a god. Now I learned my lesson, and now I knew how all those heroes in ancient tales felt. They always got screwed over by whichever god they trusted in.

Pothos, I could tell, felt a bit betrayed as well. Prometheus had been his friend and almost like a father figure. He really did think he wanted to help Chrys. In some ways he did help her. It was just that he had ulterior motives.

I swore if he laid a finger on her though… Well, I guess Chrys would kill him, not me. But I would try to get a few punches in if I could.

"Are you done yet?" Pothos asked.

I took a deep breath, the vile stench of vomit filling my nostrils. I definitely needed to rinse off and get some mint gum. "Yeah, but can we go to the store? I need to get this taste out."

"Sure, this way. I presume you don't speak Cantonese?"

I shook my head. "No."

"Well, most people speak English as well, but just in case, stick close to me. I don't want you getting lost and then not being able to communicate. We already have enough problems as it is, and although I would love to see you get in trouble with some gangs, today isn't the day." We stepped out onto the crowded street. "You can hold my hand if you want."

I gave him a look but noticed how many people there were and got a bit intimidated. I took his hand, and he smiled but didn't say anything.

He led us toward a convenience market, and I rinsed my mouth in the bathroom while he purchased some gum. We headed out as quickly as we entered, chewing gum and holding hands. Pothos swung our arms as if he was having fun.

"So where is this place?" I asked. "I presume somewhere close?"

Pothos nodded. "Yeah, just a couple more blocks."

I glanced around. It was still rather busy, even for being late at night. "Does this city ever sleep?"

"Nope, rather like your New York."

"Never been, but that's what I've heard too."

We ventured farther through the city, and I found that the types of people started to change. The longer we walked, the more people started to appear like me and the people I used to hang out with.

"Hey, Pothos, what kind of god is Aether? Because this place seems sketch."

"He's the primordial god of sky and clouds. You know ether? It's like the substance that gods live on."

So he was really important and old. "Why would he be here then?"

Pothos bit his lip. "You will see and perhaps understand. I'll just say he's a bit alluring, so to speak."

We arrived to the location, and Pothos rang the buzzer. The door opened a crack, and a woman peeked through the opening. She said something in Cantonese, and Pothos answered. I, of course, understood none of it.

The door opened fully, and we found ourselves in an area where many lay on their backs, staring up at the ceiling. All of them had pipes, or pipes near them. Everything seemed slowed and relaxed, but it made me start to fidget. The air reeked of something I wasn't quite familiar with. Was that opium? It looked like something out of a movie. Did these dens still exist?

I mean, it looked familiar to the hangouts where my

friends did drugs, except a lot nicer. It reminded me of how I died, and my heart sank a little. Would these people end up like me? Could anything save them from the torture that was to come?

I pushed back the thoughts, and Pothos pulled me to the back of the den. The girl who opened the door for us led us farther into the building and opened the door in the back. The lighting in this room was rather dark, and it took a few moments for my eyes to adjust, but when they did, I found a man sitting there, surrounded by half-naked women, either draped over him or on the ground, also enjoying the substance that everyone but us was smoking.

The man smiled, his long white hair covering his shoulders. He wore a blue robe that he tightened when he saw us enter. "Pothos, what brings you here?"

CHAPTER 9

Chrys

"Vera, what's wrong?" Circe asked as we stood in the middle of the woods. The birds were singing, and the sun was shining through the trees. It would have been perfect if it weren't for the fact I felt betrayed.

I didn't know if I could say anything to Circe and felt that the answer was probably no. She seemed close to Prometheus and Apollo, and I had a feeling she was in on this conspiracy as well. I was alone and had to find the answers for myself.

"It's nothing, just been having trouble sleeping," I said as I went back to what I was doing: looking for herbs and learning about them with Circe.

"You should have told me, dear child. I would have

made you some tea to help you sleep."

"Maybe tonight then, you could make me some and teach me about the herbs."

She nodded. "Yes, I have just the blend for you. Some valerian and passionflower with lavender and chrysanthemum."

I froze. Chrysanthemum. That seemed familiar. I remembered someone giving me that herb in a tea to help with something, but what was it?

A dull ache started to form in my head again. Ugh, when would this stop? It had to mean that something was causing me to not remember, even if I tried. What did they do to me? Who did this to me?

Was it Prometheus?

It didn't make sense that he wouldn't want me to remember anything though, unless it had something to do with him. Did he betray me? Was he just using me? Was Zeus actually the good guy in all this and Prometheus was trying to brainwash me?

I wasn't sure what I should do. I felt I should run, but to where? I was stuck on this island without anyone to help me. Part of what he said could have been true, and maybe Zeus did in fact want me dead and Prometheus didn't want me to remember something else. Then if I stepped into the water, I could be killed. There were too many factors, and I felt utterly defeated.

The only choice was to learn how to use my powers

and then figure it out from there.

"Hey, Circe, when are we going to go over the other part of my power?" I asked, trying to seem as nonchalant as I could.

"What do you mean?" she asked, a little hesitant. That indicated to me she was not someone to trust about what I heard last night.

"You had said that I had the power of life and death. So far you have shown me how to bring stuff back to life but not how my power brings the death of something. Is it like understanding the life force and instead of making it bigger to make it smaller?"

She was silent for a moment, as if trying to gather her thoughts or come up with a lie. I wasn't sure which one it was. "It's something like that. It is very strong magic, and I don't want you to get scared and for it to go out of control. First you need to learn how to calm your mind and to make sure that if you did accidentally destroy something, you'd be able to bring it back. I feel that you aren't someone who could easily destroy something and live with that fact."

That seemed pretty accurate, as the night before I had lost all control of my emotions and that was why I destroyed everything around me. I would have to be more careful next time and learn how to stay calm.

As for bringing something back from being completely destroyed, I couldn't tell her I knew how. I had brought those plants back to life last night, although the life force of a plant burned a lot differently than it did for an animal or human, or a god for that matter. I could feel the energy in the others; it was a lot stronger and a lot more powerful.

If I accidentally killed a god, would I have enough power to bring them back?

I didn't want to know the answer to that question, as I felt that power was way too much responsibility.

"What are we harvesting today?" I decided to change the subject. I did like learning about the plants and how they could help humans. Apparently Circe was one of the gods who taught humans how to heal using the plants, and she would go on and on about how most of them forgot the traditional teachings and now lived with even more sickness that could be easily remedied by relearning this wisdom.

"We are harvesting roots mainly since it is the fall. We are looking for burdock, valerian, and marshmallow."

"Marshmallow? Like the candy?" I asked, excited to see if the plant had little marshmallows growing on it. Was that how they were created?

She shook her head. "No, but the candy used to be created from the plant. It was used for throat lozenges to help with coughs and sore throats. Now it's just candy with chemicals and gelatin."

I thought it was strange that it would go from medicine to candy, but I decided not to push further. She seemed really pissed at humans for always messing things up.

We first found burdock, which was a bit strange-looking. I didn't know what I expected, but it wasn't this plant. It had large leaves that came out of the earth with flowers that were now dead and crispy.

Circe handed me a small shovel. "Start digging up the root. It has a long tap root that we want. Then we can cook with it."

"What's it taste like?" I asked as I started digging.

"A little like an earthy carrot. If you cook it just right, it will taste good. I like adding it to my broths as it is good for digestion and a healthy stomach."

I wondered what the point of keeping a healthy stomach was when we were gods and didn't have to deal with stuff like that, but I decided not to ask, as I didn't want to get scolded.

We dug up a few burdock plants, some with roots that were over two feet long. I felt that it was a great success, and we bagged the product after getting as much dirt as we could off of it.

Next we searched for valerian. In digging that up, I found it had a strong scent, almost sweet and earthy. It was definitely something one would have to get used to.

"I will make some fresh tea with this tonight for you

and it will help you go right to sleep." She smiled. "It is one of the best sedatives."

I nodded, as if I knew what she meant. It was strange to think a root like that could cause someone to sleep.

We found marshmallow and harvested the root of that. We each carried two large burlap sacks and headed back to the cottage. We would need to rinse them, slice them, and put some out to dry and then use burdock in some broth and in some other recipes. I was excited to try it.

It took a couple of hours to process everything, but once it was done, I felt pretty successful. It was productive, and I could even make peace with doing this for the rest of my life. But I knew that wasn't my fate, and I had much more pressing matters to tend to.

Circe started preparing for that night's meal when I decided to ask for some free time. I wanted to be able to think alone, and it seemed that they were giving me a little more freedom, as long as I followed their rules.

"Circe," I said. "Can I go out in the woods and meditate? I feel closer to the earth now, processing all this, and I want to finish the day off with a meditation." It wasn't a lie, but I knew if I worded it like that, she would be more inclined to let me.

She smiled. "Sure thing, Vera, just make sure you get back here by dark, okay? Food will be ready by then."

I nodded and hurried off into the woods. I was glad

she trusted me, but I could see Prometheus and Apollo eye me as I headed out. I hadn't said much to them since last night, and I really didn't want to try to hide the fact I had heard them. It was best if I just tried to avoid them for the time being.

Heading into the woods, I let the scenery take me in. It was beautiful on this island, and I couldn't believe that it was already fall. It felt so much warmer than that. The reminder that it was fall brought an itchy feeling to my head. What was it about fall that made me worry? What made me uneasy? Whatever it was, it wasn't coming to me.

I was surprised that Apollo was in the cottage too, as he usually disappeared during the day and came back before night. He had mentioned something about his sister seeing him in the moonlight. What did he mean by that? And why was he avoiding her?

And what was the talk about him being a wolf?

I hated how everything felt familiar yet also distant. It was like seeing the water out in the ocean but not being able to understand what was going on below the surface. I just wanted to look, but something was keeping me from doing that.

As I kept on walking, I found myself nearing the other side of the island. Had I really been walking that long? Circe said it took a good three hours to walk all the way across the island. Maybe I somehow got turned around and had veered on my path toward the right or left edges of the island. I looked up at the sky and found that seemed more likely.

Looking out at the ocean, I took a deep breath. I loved the smell of the salty air and the cool breeze that came from it.

That was when I heard them—those singing creatures that kept drawing me toward the ocean. I tried to turn away and run into the woods before it was too late, but they already had me in their grasp.

And this time there was no one to stop me.

The soothing melody made me alert and sleepy all at the same time. It was almost like it was directing me but in a way where I didn't know what I was doing and I couldn't change my mind. I stepped closer and closer to the water until finally I was only a couple of inches from it.

I took one step into the water, and something grabbed me by the ankle and dragged me under.

CHAPTER 10

Huntley

Something about being in an opium den was weird. We were meeting a god, right? I guess most of the gods did drugs like this, but I was expecting a little more refinement from Aether since he was older. After all this time, however, I shouldn't have been surprised by Aether's indulgent behavior.

He was still sitting in front of us, waiting for Pothos to respond. The half-naked women stayed where they were, tracing Aether's skin with their fingers, clearly high on this opium. The scent of burnt sugar filled my nostrils. It was a lot different than the vinegar stench I had been used to.

I guess that was the difference between a fancy parlor

and whatever kids could get their hands on off the street.

Noting my hands begin to shake, I tried to ignore the itching feeling that was starting to cover my body. I knew not to start scratching my skin, as that wasn't the problem. Even though I had died and even though I was revived by Chrys, the yearning was still there. Luckily, I hadn't been in the presence of any drug for a long while, but now it surrounded me and my body wanted a taste, which would lead to more than just a taste, and just like the people we saw in the entry, I would be a slave to this drug.

I held on to the image of Chrys. I could be strong for her. I was clean—I hadn't had anything for years, except the pomegranates, but that was different. Apparently.

"I heard that Prometheus visited you not too long ago. Do you have any idea where he could have gone?" Pothos asked, ignoring everything else going on in this room.

Aether placed his pipe on his lips and took in a puff. He breathed it out slowly. "And what made you think I would know?"

"My brothers told me. So don't lie. You know I can see what's in your heart."

He laughed. "If you can see what's in someone's heart, then you should have known Prometheus was up to his old shenanigans."

Pothos pursed his lips. Aether had a point, and I wondered why Pothos hadn't noticed.

"Prometheus was good at hiding his true intentions. He's able to hide his heart from me. I thought I could trust him, but apparently I was wrong. I have learned my lesson. Now please, you have to help or Olympus could be in trouble."

Aether motioned to the girls, and they got up and moved so he could stand. As he stood, I found that he was taller than he appeared. His robe opened a little, and I could see the muscles on his chest and abs. Even if he were human and didn't have powers, there would be no way I would even get a punch in. I stepped toward Pothos, a little afraid now.

"Why should I tell you?" he asked with a slight smile as he noted my fear. "Maybe I want Olympus taken down a notch. It's not like I have any ties to Zeus."

"All the gods are at risk, and you know it." Pothos looked him square in the eyes. "You will be in danger as well if Prometheus wants to be the most powerful."

Aether took a puff of his pipe again and blew it in our faces. It was sweet and fragrant, and I wished he would offer me just a taste. My body started to itch even more. I scratched my arm, trying to distract myself from the scent. I couldn't be tempted—I couldn't fall down that path again when I needed to find Chrys.

As I tried to turn myself away from the scent, I noticed Aether's eyes move to me. "And what do we have here? A human?"

Before I could say anything, Pothos answered. "He's Chrys's husband. He may be human, but he is strong."

"Oh really now? The daughter of Hades is married to a human? I bet Hades loves that." He laughed a little. He held out his pipe. "But I can tell you want some, don't you?"

I stared at the pipe. It was there for the taking. Would a taste really hurt? I started to reach out for it, in a trance of its pleasure and beauty. Another image of Chrys came to my mind, and I was able to pull back my hand. "That is not why we are here. Answer our question: Where is Prometheus?"

Turning, Aether traced his finger along the side of one girl's face. I felt bad for them, as I could tell they were trapped in the haze that was this drug. Were they human? Or were they something else? I tried not to think about it—it wasn't why we were there.

But it did remind me of my own demons.

"Prometheus had a few places in mind and came to me to get a location that he didn't believe Zeus could ever find."

"And what place is that?" Pothos asked.

Aether took a puff. "He was looking for where the witch resides."

Pothos pinched the bridge of his nose. "Fuck."

"Fuck indeed."

"What is it? What witch?" I asked. It seemed that Pothos knew who he was talking about, which was good, but I didn't like his frown.

Pothos turned to me. "Circe. She is known to be a loner and not to be disturbed. No one knows where she lives, although it is definitely on an island somewhere. But the location of the island has been a secret for centuries."

"Why would she let Prometheus on her island then? If she doesn't like people."

"Because Chrys could bring about the destruction of Olympus and destroy the gods she hates. Mainly Zeus."

Aether smiled. "Seems you have one hell of a wife. Everyone wants her on their side."

I shot him a look.

Pothos turned to Aether. "Do you know where the island is?"

He shrugged. "I've had guesses, but I am not sure I would want to give that information to you."

"Zeus will be right on our tail. If he sees we paid you a visit, he will be knocking on your door soon," Pothos said.

"Zeus knows not to mess with me. We have had our differences in the past, and it was decided we'd stay out of each other's hair. No matter what the situation is."

I couldn't believe what I was hearing. He knew where to find Chrys, yet he wouldn't give us the information. We were back where we started, except this time I was looking straight at the god who could put an end to this.

I wanted to kill him.

"Human, you seem angry. Let me explain something to you: we gods have lived for centuries upon centuries and then some. We have our rules, and we have our reasons. You cannot comprehend our life. Giving up information like this isn't so simple." He took a puff of his pipe and sat down. Some of the girls returned to his lap. "You have a long way to go before you understand the things that are going on around this universe."

Something in me snapped. I guess I was just sick of these gods being so full of themselves and only caring about their ego that I just couldn't deal with it anymore. I rushed toward him and grabbed him by the collar of his robe. The girls moved out of the way but didn't scream as they were too affected by the drug.

"Oh, you think you are scary? How cute." Aether blew smoke in my face.

"Look, I am sick of all this! You think Zeus will just follow your truce? When has Zeus ever followed anything? He just thinks about himself, just like all of you!"

Pothos stepped forward. "Huntley, I think you should

—"

"No! I am done playing nice with you lot! The love of my life has been kidnapped, and who knows what he is doing to her! If Zeus finds her first, she is dead! I can't let that happen!"

Aether blew more smoke into my face. I was getting a little sick and tired of it, but he just smiled. "You have guts. I like it. But unfortunately, I truly don't know where Circe is. No one but Prometheus and now Apollo does. I wasn't able to give him that information, just a way to bring her out. And that way isn't going to work since she is hiding from you all for a reason now."

So this was just another dead end. Fuck.

"How did he get her off the island?" Pothos asked. "I mean, it's worth a shot."

"No, he got to her by placing a rare herb in the water and waited till it reached her shore. Then she came looking to see where it came from."

"Which herb?"

"Moly, ironically. It used to grow on her island, and it was used to deceive her. She destroyed it all so no human could deceive her again. I have no idea how Prometheus found the plant, but she feared there was more and went searching for it, and that's how Prometheus found her."

Great, Prometheus had ties everywhere. He must have been weaving this web for longer than we even realized. No wonder he was able to deceive everyone, even Pothos.

"Now, I've given you all the information I have. Do with it what you want, but just please leave. You are starting to kill my high. That is, unless you want to join." He smiled at me.

I did, but I wasn't going to admit it to him. I let go of his robe and turned to Pothos. He nodded and we headed out. The first thing I did when we got outside was take a few deep breaths of fresh air and bend over, trying to control my body from jumping back in there to get more.

Pothos placed his hand on my back but didn't say a word. I felt that he understood and knew what I was going through. After a few moments, he removed his hand.

"I'm going to call Hades and tell him what we have found. We don't need to go to the other locations but need to focus on finding Circe."

I nodded as he took out his phone and called Hades. I closed my eyes and took another deep breath.

We were getting closer, but I felt we still had a long way to go. I just wanted it to be over, was that too much to ask?

"He says to meet him back at the flat in London and then we are going to split up again. Luckily, Persephone already sent out the sirens, so if any of them step into the water, we will know it. Circe, Apollo, and Prometheus won't hear the song, but they might have told her to stay away from the water."

I straightened up and nodded. "Yeah, we can only hope."

CHAPTER 11

Chrys

In an instant, I found my entire body under the water. Wasn't I just on the beach? How did I find myself here?

The water was warm, and I tried to move around but panicked a little and didn't want to open my eyes. I was too afraid of the consequences and what I had done. Prometheus had told me not to go into the water, and yet that song dragged me into it. I couldn't escape it, no matter how hard I tried.

Was this how I would die? After everything, was the water going to consume me and I would perish without knowing the truth of my past?

Deciding to finally face the inevitable, I opened my eyes. It took a moment for them to adjust to the clear blue water. To my surprise, I found a woman swimming in front of me. Her hand was wrapped around my ankle, her red hair floating perfectly in the water. I glanced down to find her lower body was that of a fish. What was she? Was she working for Zeus? Was she going to take me to him to be killed? Or was she just going to drown me herself?

After going down pretty far into the water, she stopped and turned to me. Her face was beautiful like porcelain. If I didn't know better, I would think she wasn't living but actually a doll. I watched her blue eyes look me over. They were as clear as the sea.

I was at my breaking point. I could no longer hold my breath and started gasping. Water filled my lungs, and I began to choke. In my struggle, the half-fish woman grabbed the sides of my face and put her pink lips to mine.

Shocked, I didn't do anything. Why was she kissing me? What the heck? I didn't struggle, as I didn't understand what was going on and knew it would be worse if I struggled.

Then I could feel the water being pulled out of my lungs and I could breathe again.

She backed away and smiled. "Can you talk now?"

Was she crazy? There was no way I would be able to talk underwater. I gave it a shot though, as I didn't have anything to lose.

"Yes?" To my surprise, I could talk. I touched my mouth. How was that possible?

"Great. My name is Thelia. I am a siren."

Suddenly two more sirens appeared next to me. I screamed a little, surprised. They appeared similar to the first woman, all with red hair and ocean-blue eyes.

"Your mother sent us to look for you. We've been scouring the sky and seas, sending out our siren song to enchant you." The younger looking of the three swam around me. "The name is Peisy and this is Aggie."

I nodded, as if their names seemed familiar. They didn't, but there was something else they said that I wanted to know more about.

"My mother? What do you mean my mother?"

Peisy nodded. "Yes, Persephone. And your father is worried sick. I have never seen him look so scared."

My father? So Prometheus had lied to me? Or were these creatures lying to me?

"You mean Prometheus?" I asked. "Isn't he my father?"

Peisy shook her head, a little confused. "No, that is the man who kidnapped you. Hades is your father, of course."

"Didn't Persephone say that they gave her a vial of Lethe? Can she not remember anything?" Aggie asked.

"That's right. Do you remember who you are?" Thelia looked me over, a little worried.

I shook my head. "I can't remember anything."

Thelia grabbed my wrist. "Come with us and we will keep you safe. We have to get you to your mother and father to figure this out."

I tried to pull away, and she didn't resist. "No, I don't know if you are telling the truth. Prometheus said he was my father and that the creatures in the ocean were taking me to Zeus to be killed."

Thelia shook her head. "No, we aren't working for Zeus. Prometheus was the one who kidnapped you. Although Zeus is after you too, and he is also after Prometheus for taking you and using you to try to kill him. That was why he erased your memories. Everything is a complicated mess, but if we can get you to Hades, we will be able to figure it all out."

Everything all of a sudden felt like it was swirling around in my head. I didn't know if they were telling the truth or if Prometheus was telling the truth and these sirens were trying to trick me into going with them and would give me over.

"Come on, we have to go before it is too late," Thelia said as she pulled my wrist.

"No, I can't. I don't know what's going on." My head was pounding now. Hades? Persephone? Was all this true? Was that why Prometheus didn't want me to remember—otherwise I would know he was lying?

"Chrys, please, hurry!"

She called me by the name Prometheus had said. Maybe they did know the truth. Maybe they were the ones I could trust.

I held out my hand just as something hit me straight in the stomach, almost like a sword, and I felt it drag me down farther and farther into the ocean.

"Chrys!" the sirens screamed as they swam after me.

I hit the bottom of the ocean and finally could focus on what the pain was coming from. A large trident was stuck in my stomach.

What the hell was this? I tried to move it, but it wouldn't even budge. I struggled as I watched red color wisp through the water. More and more blood was pouring out of me.

I watched as a figure came closer to me, and I finally was able to make out the silhouette of a man. He held out his hand, and the trident released me from the ocean floor and went into his hand.

"Well what do we have here?" The dark, curly-haired man smiled.

CHAPTER 12

Huntley

After throwing up a bit in the bathroom, I headed back into the living room where the rest of the gods discussed what to do next. I had a feeling Pothos already went over what Aether had said to them. By the time I got to the living room, Hades was already seated, pinching the bridge of his nose.

"Circe hasn't been seen in centuries. There is no way to find her without getting any of them to go into the ocean." He took a long deep breath. "I'm going to kill Prometheus."

Persephone placed her hand on his back. "My sirens are sending out their song to her. She will more than likely go into the water, and we will know where she is."

Hades shook his head. "Prometheus will know we would send the sirens. He will tell her not to go into the water."

"If she goes into the water, though, my father will know right away as well," AJ interjected. "And I doubt your sirens would be any match for them."

A knife appeared in Hades's hand, and he threw it straight at AJ's throat. I tried not to look as blood gushed out of the wound. Pothos sighed, as he had to now bleach his carpet again. Mel walked over and started wiping the blood off AJ's face with a small, sadistic smile. She really liked her new toy.

"Chrys can handle herself against Poseidon. She has done it before," I said.

Hades stood up with a sigh. "I am not worried about Poseidon as much as I am about Zeus being able to tell where she is. We have to find her before he does."

We were all silent, in agreement that the goal was to find her before Zeus did. If Poseidon found her, it would only be moments before Zeus knew as well. If that happened, then we were royally screwed.

"Is there any way to find Circe? I mean, we know Prometheus did it using some kind of flower. Maybe we could do something like that?"

Hades shook his head. "No, she knows we are looking for her and will stay hidden. She will see this as the only way to take down Olympus, and she will seize the opportunity. Her and Zeus aren't exactly on the best terms."

"Is anyone on the best terms with Zeus?" Pothos asked as he sat down on the ground and leaned against the wall.

"Well, apparently enough people still fear him since there isn't any who will side with us." Hades pinched the bridge of his nose again, as if trying to relieve a headache. "Apparently they fear him more than they fear me in the Underworld."

"So we are back where we started. We just have to eliminate possibilities of where the island would be, right?" I went over to the map. "We just start searching."

"Huntley, the island is mystical. Unless you know exactly where it is, you can't find it."

I smacked my head on the wall. "Why is this always more complicated than it needs to be?"

"Welcome to why I don't deal with anything outside the Underworld." Hades stood up. "And why I hate dealing with all these other gods."

Persephone took a seat on the couch. "We will figure this out. She's strong and will be able to take care of herself until we get to her."

Hades turned to her, and I could tell he was on the edge of breaking. "She's on that island with Prometheus and Apollo! Who knows what they have done to her!"

I didn't like it when Hades started to lose it—he was usually the one who stayed calm in these situations. It made me worry even more.

"Circe is there. She wouldn't let harm come to a maiden, okay?" Persephone tried to calm him down. "That was why she has been hiding herself from the gods all this time."

"What is her story? I mean, why would Prometheus look for her during all this?" I asked.

Persephone let out a sigh. "Well, that goes back a few centuries, but to put it simply—she's free. Zeus doesn't like free people and tried to suppress her, but that didn't end well. She found an island, hid, and turns any human who finds her island into animals."

"As to why she would help Prometheus"—Hades took a deep breath—"he probably promised her Zeus's demise, and then she could be as free as she wanted and return her knowledge to the world."

"Knowledge?" I asked. "What kind of knowledge?"

Mel answered as she traced her knife on AJ's jeans. "Herbal medicine, plants, potions, magick. All the stuff that was lost to the world, or at least mostly lost. She was the original witch, so to speak."

There didn't seem to be anything wrong with that, or at least I didn't think so. Then again, I was sure some exes I knew would use powers to curse some people, so maybe it was bad. But that wasn't the problem.

"So Chrys is helping so she can be free of Zeus. I presume Apollo is the same. We are trying to get Chrys, and everyone else is staying out of it," I reiterated.

"That is pretty much it. Most of it has to do with Zeus. We need to be faster than Zeus and Poseidon and then we can hide her in the Underworld, and that would give us enough time until Zeus gets bored and forgets about it all," Hades said.

Pothos commented, "Aether said he wouldn't tell Zeus what he knows, so we have that going for us. I doubt Zeus would push him, even given the circumstances. He could easily bring Olympus to its knees. Kinda wish he would though."

Hades retorted, "Zeus just might find out on his own. But either way, he doesn't know where Circe is. There has to be someone who knows where she is."

Persephone shook her head. "No, if anyone knew, then her place would be compromised. Everyone would have known by now."

"So we just have to wait?" I asked. "And hope the sirens are able to call her out?"

Hades took a deep breath and collapsed on the couch. "It looks like it. I still don't understand why Apollo went along with it though."

Persephone shook her head. "No, that's an easy answer. He just wanted a little chaos, not to mention he doesn't care for Zeus. He wants to be able to goof off more, and if Prometheus gets his wish, he will let Apollo do whatever he wants."

Hades shook his head as he leaned forward with his elbows on his knees. "He's such a bastard. First he tried to win you over—when we were married no less—and then now this. I swear, if he lays a finger on her…"

Pothos was the one to answer. "Don't worry. Apollo isn't stupid enough to try anything with a girl who can destroy him and send him to Tartarus. Plus they want her to trust them and do their bidding. That would sabotage everything."

Hades let out a sigh. "I suppose you are right. I still can't help but worry."

Persephone placed her hand on his back. "We are all worried. But she will be okay as long as we get to her first."

"That's the thing. Will we? I am starting to have my doubts."

"What…," I began, not sure if I should ask, "happens if Zeus finds her first. I mean, like, what exactly can he do?"

Hades didn't look at me but looked down at the ground. "He will send her to Tartarus where she will be tormented for an eternity."

Tartarus. The real hell of stories and legends. I had seen it with my own eyes as souls fell and fell and fell. I couldn't imagine, nor did I want to.

"Is there any way you could get her out of there? If Zeus did succeed, I mean."

Hades was quiet for a moment. "There are ways, but…"

Persephone intervened. "No, there isn't any way. Not without releasing the titans that will destroy this world and Olympus and the Underworld. Everything will be destroyed, so either way it wouldn't matter, would it, Hades?"

"You're right. There is no way we can release anyone from Tartarus. It would mean the end of everything."

Great, so there was no backup plan. I didn't even want to think about what those titans were like. "Isn't Prometheus a titan?"

Mel answered. "He is… but he isn't as powerful as Kronos and the others. Just like there are some gods who are more powerful, he got the bad end of the stick."

I shrugged. "Seems to me he got the good side since he is still alive while the others are tormented for an eternity."

Pothos let out a laugh. "I suppose you are right in that instance. Good for you, Huntley."

I shot him a look. "Hey, I'm smarter than I look, and you know it!"

Pothos kept on laughing, and I noticed even Hades

made a smile, but it was a brief moment before the room went back to a quiet, miserable mess. I glanced out the window where the storm was still raging on.

I prayed the sirens would find her and we would finally be out of this mess.

CHAPTER 13

Chrys

"Looks like a little bitch stumbled into my domain."

That man who stood above me peered down with such hatred in his eyes. Was this Zeus? Was he going to kill me? I glanced over at the trident that was now in his hand. No, something about this didn't feel right—he didn't seem like he would be Zeus. But that didn't mean he didn't want to kill me.

I felt as if I had seen him before, but I couldn't put together all the details. I remembered being in the water and him dragging me somewhere, then everything went black. Was this really a memory, or were things too jumbled in my head? Pain shot through my head, and I decided right now was not the time to figure that out.

Trying to move, I found that not only did my head hurt, but so did the rest of my body. Blood was still floating out of my body and mixing with the water. This was bad—I needed to do something about these wounds.

Then it hit me—could I heal myself like I had healed that deer? I shut my eyes and focused on the wounds and commanded them to heal by drawing energy from different parts of my body. When I opened my eyes, I found that the wounds had been healed.

How powerful was I?

Glancing back up, I found the man smirking. "You are going to pay for what you did to me a year ago. I was the laughingstock of Olympus. Now you will die by my hand."

"I don't know what I did, but do you think we can talk about it?"

He raised an eyebrow. "You don't remember?"

I shook my head. "No, I have no idea who you are or who I am for that matter."

The man let out a hearty laugh. "Well, isn't this cute? How about this? I will introduce myself. I am Poseidon, god of the seas, and I am going to be the one who kills you and presents you to Zeus."

He raised his trident, and I closed my eyes, waiting for the worst. I didn't know how I could escape a god as powerful as this, and he wasn't even Zeus. I still didn't have my answers, and I would die not knowing who I was.

This just sucked.

Before Poseidon could attack, I heard one of the sirens call out to him.

"Poseidon! Don't! It wasn't her fault what happened a year ago but more your own arrogance! If you hadn't tried to kidnap her, she wouldn't have hurt you!"

I opened my eyes to find all three of them pulling back his arm so he couldn't stab me.

He shook his head. "Out of my way, you vile creatures!"

"No, we swore an oath to Persephone that we would keep her daughter safe!" Thelia exclaimed.

"And we will not go back on our word!" Aggie exclaimed.

"Do you think you would be able to stop me? You are nothing compared to my power! Don't make me destroy you too!" Poseidon yanked the trident out of their grip and pointed it at me. "If I don't destroy her, Zeus will. You think Hades will be able to hide her in the Underworld? That is not going to be possible. She is dead one way or another."

"It was Prometheus who betrayed Zeus, not her! She has shown she wouldn't hurt anyone unless provoked, yet you gods keep provoking her!" Thelia explained as she got between me and Poseidon.

"She has the potential to turn on us and destroy Olympus. I will not have that!"

Thelia turned her head a little toward me. "Men do not listen, do they?"

I didn't know what was going on. Why were so many of them after me? What did I do before I'd forgotten my memories? These sirens claimed Prometheus had given me something to wipe my memories and had kidnapped me. They were protecting me from Poseidon. Were they then telling me the truth? Were Hades and Persephone my real parents? And if so, was my name really Chrys?

What the hell was going on?

My head started pounding, and I grabbed my head.

"Everything just needs to stop!" I screamed. "Leave me alone! I just want to be left alone!" I could feel the energy inside ebb. It was black, dark, and cold, and I felt it seeping out of me just like it had done the night before.

Except this time that energy was a lot larger. I wrapped my arms around myself and took deep breaths. What would happen if I lost all control? I didn't want to find out the hard way and tried my best to hold it in.

"Move!" Poseidon raised his trident as Thelia stood in front of me. "Or you will just get killed in the process!"

Thelia held out her arms. "Never!"

"Very well."

Poseidon threw his trident, and it hit her straight in the chest. She gasped and blood began to cloud the area. It was more blood than I believed I had ever seen. Thelia's body swayed in the water, her life gone. I tried to reach out for her—tried to focus on bringing the life back—but I was still having trouble holding all the dark energy in myself. If I didn't focus on that, then everyone there would die in an instant.

I couldn't save her.

"Thelia!" The other sirens screamed. I felt their sorrow, making the dark energy in me expand. I shook my head and held myself close. I couldn't let it go or the other sirens would meet a similar fate.

Poseidon advanced toward me, but it was taking all my focus to stop from destroying everything in this ocean. Aggie swam in front of me, and I watched as she met the same fate as Thelia. I screamed as I watched Peisy turn and swim away as fast as she could. I didn't blame her— she needed to get out of there before she met the same fate.

Now that just left Poseidon and me. He smiled, as if satisfied that he now had just me in his clutches.

"Well, now I guess not even the daughter of Hades has people who can save her."

My head was screaming now, with images of a man with dark hair. Was that my father? Was that Hades?

I shook my head. "I don't remember anything. What

did I do to you? Who am I? What is going on?"

He laughed. "It seems that Lethe is quite powerful stuff. It is said to be liquid henbane, as the plant grows along the river. It can destroy your memories or make you have a directive, as seen with Hercules. I'm surprised it would have such an effect on the daughter of Hades herself. Then again, I heard Prometheus gave you a whole bottle when only a few drops are needed. He must have really wanted to make sure you didn't remember."

Prometheus was behind all this. Poseidon had no reason to lie, not when he was about to kill me. He had acted like he was my father. He gave me another name and was using me to destroy Olympus.

Everything was a lie.

Well, everything except the fact it seemed everyone wanted to kill me. At least I could hold on to that.

Poseidon grabbed me by the throat. "Now, hold still while I send you to your death."

I shut my eyes and released all the power that had been forming inside me. I didn't care if anything else got in the way at that point.

Poseidon was struck by the black lightning that had been released from my body. His body shook as all of it went into him. Something was different this time, however. When it happened before, I had felt everything expand from my body, and while that was still happening this time, I also felt energy coming from Poseidon at the same time.

I was killing him and absorbing his energy.

What happened when I absorbed it all? Would he be dead? Would he go to the Underworld? Will I have won? Or would even more people be after me?

I didn't want to be a killer, but Poseidon had left me no choice. If I didn't end him now, he would keep trying to destroy me—that much I could tell. I had apparently attacked him before, and he had held a grudge. I couldn't let him go this time.

As I sat too deep in my thoughts, Poseidon was able to raise his trident and stab me in the stomach. The surprise attack caused me to falter and Poseidon was able to back away from me and out of reach of my dark power.

Well, shit.

I was able to heal quickly since I was taking energy from him. Poseidon leaned against his trident, his eyes dark with rage. He was breathing heavily and tried to gather up what strength he had.

"I won't let you get away with almost killing me again. You do not deserve to have that power! No one does!"

"But you are trying to kill me! I wouldn't be using it if I weren't in danger all the time!"

"I am a god of Olympus! I can do what I like and

shouldn't have to fear for my death. You shouldn't be able to harm us. Your father knew this, yet he hid you for so long. He should be tried for his crimes as well, but I know that will never happen. He gets away with shit like this all the time."

I had no idea what he was talking about, and I wasn't sure if that was more frustrating or the fact I couldn't get Poseidon to stop attacking me.

Now that I had so much of his energy in me, I knew it wouldn't take much to kill him. His attacks were slow as he tried to stab me again and again with the trident, but I quickly moved out of the way.

However, with every pressing second, I could feel his power start to rise more and more. He must have had some kind of healing ability. I needed to act fast.

I raised my hand and gathered the dark energy once more, letting it take over my entire body.

"No, you don't!" Poseidon yelled as he charged me, his trident ready to stab me once more.

He pinned me against the large rocks that stood at the bottom of the ocean. I couldn't move.

Raising his hand, he drew from the power of the ocean. "This is the end, daughter of Hades. Any last words?"

No, that couldn't be the end. I wouldn't let it. I let out a scream that blasted energy every which way, destroying the rock, destroying the life, and everything

within meters of myself.
  Including Poseidon.

CHAPTER 14

Huntley

Hades stood up fast, as if he saw something outside. I glanced out the window, not spotting anything except the wrathful storm.

"What is it, sweetie?" Persephone asked.

"I sense… Chrys. Something is happening but I can't figure out where. She is fighting someone using…" He hurried to his coat. "We have to figure out who it is before Zeus notices as well. With that much power being used, he is going to notice."

Mel turned to the window. "I sense it too. Great darkness, just like last time."

Just like last time. I glanced out the window but didn't notice anything. I wasn't a god though, and she was probably miles upon miles away. But that didn't mean I didn't feel helpless. I was supposed to her husband, and I couldn't even tell whatever was going on. I couldn't figure out where she was.

Maybe the others were right—maybe a human like me couldn't be in love with a goddess—I would be too powerless to stop anything from happening.

I shook my head. No, I wouldn't give up. I would do anything for her, and I didn't care if I was human—I could still help her in ways these gods couldn't.

What way that was, I still wasn't sure. But I would figure it out. I had to.

Persephone stood up, but she didn't gather her things. "Hades, you don't know where she is. You can't help her. If she is fighting who you think she is, we would know. My sirens would come get us."

Hades shook his head. "Your sirens can't do anything against Poseidon. You think he would let them escape? No, that power meant he is fighting my daughter. I have to go find her or—" He stopped, not wanting to say the end. "I have to go. You can stay here just in case the sirens come back, but I need to act faster. Call me if any of them managed to survive."

He opened the door, and I quickly grabbed my own jacket. "Let me come with you."

"No, it's too dangerous."

"If she doesn't remember you, she is going to be

scared. You know how she gets when her emotions overrun her mind. I can help her."

He took a deep breath. "If she can't remember me, how would you be able to stop her? She wouldn't remember you nor her love for you."

Hades had a point. I didn't know how to respond.

"Take him with you." Persephone sighed. "You know as well as I how love can do the impossible. Maybe Huntley will be able to get her to remember who she is."

Hades flared his nostrils. "Fine, but if you die, it's not my fault. Her power will send you to Tartarus, and I can't do anything to stop that."

I nodded and hurried after him as we stepped out into the pouring rain. Lightning flashed in the sky and thunder quickly followed suit. Zeus still hadn't let up after all these days. The streets were gathering water, and I was surprised some of those cars still could move around in it. It was said to be the worst flooding England—and Europe—had ever had.

"Why are we outside? Why don't we use the portal?" I asked.

Hades didn't say anything but rounded a corner and disappeared. Shit, did I lose him? I walked around the same area he did, and suddenly I was somewhere warm. There were birds chirping in the distance.

What the hell?

I glanced around to find Hades walking away. Did he just assume I would figure that portal out? I hurried after, realizing that my stomach didn't hurt. What the heck? What was that? I started to open my mouth to say something but decided not to. Hades was driven by love for his daughter, and I did not want to interfere. It took all my effort to keep up with him.

Taking another look around, we had to be somewhere in the Mediterranean. There were Greek letters on all the signs, plentiful sunshine, white clay buildings, and a beach as far as the eyes could see. It felt like an island though, so where were we?

Hades hurried to the water and stopped, staring out at, one could only assume, where he thought Chrys was.

Suddenly the water became restless, waves growing bigger and bigger, and the clouds formed, becoming almost as black as night. The humans who were around quickly got up and headed indoors as they saw the storm approach. If I didn't want to lose sight of Hades, I would have joined them. These clouds rolling in were worse than those that covered London's sky.

A large bolt of lightning hit the sand, nearly blinding me, and the thunder pierced my ears.

"Jesus Christ!" I fell back, rubbing my eyes. "What the—"

"Hades!" a loud voice yelled before me. "Where is she?"

My eyes were able to focus now, and I found Zeus standing in front of us. I quickly turned to Hades, who had a stiff jaw as he glared at his brother.

"Well? Do not disobey me, brother! I do not have time to deal with you." Lightning crackled in Zeus's hand. I scrambled back on my hands and knees. There was no way I would survive an attack from him, even with Hades there.

Hades growled. "I do not know where she is. Like you, I felt the energy surge and have come looking for her. She is in trouble, and I have a feeling our brother is to blame. It is not her fault he has put her in a position to defend herself. And this isn't the first time either."

Zeus ignored the comment. "She is a threat to all of us. She needs to be destroyed!"

"I will never let you hurt her! It is not her fault she is being used by Prometheus! It is him you should punish, not her!"

I kept my mouth shut. I did not want to get in the middle of this argument.

"She is too powerful! You see what happens when she loses control? Why aren't you seeing what is right in front of you!"

"Because she can control her powers if you just leave her alone! Everything she has done has been in self-defense! If you just let her stay in the Underworld with me, she wouldn't cause harm to any of you!"

It wasn't always self-defense, as she sometimes had outbursts in the Underworld, but I wasn't going to bring that up. She also did it when she was angry. I took a few more steps back as I saw Hades start to gather power.

"You are unwise to defy me. I know you want revenge for sticking you in the Underworld, and you have trained your daughter to take me down."

"You are mistaken. The Underworld has been a blessing as it has kept me away from all of you! If I didn't have my solitude, I would have probably snapped and killed you all ages ago."

A couple more steps back. At that point, the humans that had been on the beach were long gone, disappearing after the lightning struck. They weren't stupid Americans—they used to believe in these gods. They could tell that shit was going down.

Darkness began to swell around Hades like it had around Chrys many times. This was different though, as it was controlled and so much darker. I had seen Hades fight once before, but seeing it again was surreal. He always had such a calm composure that one forgot how dangerous he really was.

I was so glad he never decided to get truly mad at me.

Zeus retaliated and summoned even more energy around him. Lightning lashed out and crashed all around him, and I took even more steps back. It was as if all the energy in the sky was now swirling around him.

Well, shit.

I knew I needed to stop it—I knew they needed to stop arguing and focus on trying to find Chrys. However, if Zeus found Chrys first, he might kill her. That was why Hades wanted to fight then and there, before his daughter was discovered.

But if Hades lost, then everything would be over. Chrys would be killed, and I would be without her. No, I couldn't let Hades hurt himself. Not after everything.

"Hades, wait!" I called after him. "You can't fight him, not like this!"

He turned and glared at me. "This is not your fight. You are a human, so leave me be!"

I knew he had a point, but that didn't mean I wasn't right. "If you lose, Chrys won't stand a chance against Zeus. You have to wait until we find her!"

Hades growled. "I can't let that bastard kill her! I have to stop him now!"

I knew I was going to regret saying the next part. "But were you ever able to defeat him earlier? No! He is more powerful than you, just admit it!"

I've had my fair share of glares and looks from Hades, but this was probably the worst of all of them. He looked as if he wanted to send me to Tartarus right then and there. And he just might.

"What did you just say?"

I was quiet for a moment, when my cell phone started to buzz. I checked it; it was Pothos. Thank the gods, I was saved.

"What's up?" I answered the phone, turning away from Hades before he could kill me.

"Is Hades with you?" he asked.

"Yeah, why? What did you find?"

"Persephone has been trying to call him. One of the sirens was able to make it back. Poseidon killed the other two… She escaped as Chrys started fighting Poseidon. She knows where the island is."

"Where is she?"

I realized I said that a little too loud and caught Zeus's attention. In a flash, he was next to me and grabbed the phone.

"Where is Chrys?" he asked.

I wished I could hear what Pothos said.

"Tell me now, or I will come and send you all to Tartarus!"

Zeus was silent for a moment and let out a breath. "Hades can't save you if I've already sent you into the depths of Tartarus. Even he can't pull out souls from there. Now tell me!"

A couple of seconds passed and Zeus's lips curled into a smile. "Now was that so hard?"

Zeus hung up the phone and smiled. "Seems I have the location of Circe's island, and you"—he crunched the phone in his hand—"have nothing."

Zeus vanished a moment later. I turned to Hades, who let out a sigh as he pulled out his buzzing phone.

"He's not the brightest, is he?" Hades murmured as he answered. "Where is she, Persephone?" He hung up the phone and turned to me. "We have no time to waste. Just promise not to throw up on me."

CHAPTER 15

Chrys

The dead body of Poseidon floated in the water in front of me.

I had calmed down enough now that I could stop unleashing so much power and death. All the underwater life around me was destroyed, and a powerful god was dead. I did this—all this was because of me.

Death surrounded me, and I felt as if it were a curse. Maybe Poseidon was right—maybe no one should have this power. But I didn't choose it. What was I supposed to do?

I could bring things back from the dead, as I had been practicing with Circe all this time, but do I do that to

Poseidon—the god who had tried so desperately to kill me? No, that would be a bad choice to make. He had mentioned that I had used my power on him before, and that was probably what I had done.

Just out of curiosity, I reached out to see if there was any energy—any spark—left in him. There was nothing. I couldn't bring him back even if I wanted to.

I could kill one of the most powerful gods without any trouble.

I was in deep shit—I was in terrible deep shit. I had to get back to the island and tell the others what had happened. It wasn't like I could swim somewhere else, not to mention the other siren had run off. Hopefully there was help on the way, unless they too were going to betray me.

No, they had sacrificed their lives for me. There was no way the others would tell Zeus.

My best bet was telling Circe and Prometheus everything.

They had lied to me, and I understood that now. I had to work to find my memories, but in the meantime, I knew they were going to keep me safe from whatever was coming. They had risked everything to kidnap me, so I knew they wouldn't turn on me now.

The problem was, I was on the bottom of the ocean with no idea about how to get back.

Closing my eyes, I focused on the island. Maybe I

had the power to figure out how to get there. I took a deep breath, which was still weird to do underwater, but the sirens made it possible.

As I listened to the ocean around me, I realized I had no idea where the island was to begin with. I didn't know how big this world was or how I was to navigate it. I tried to focus on something—focused on Circe and the others. Perhaps I could sense their energy, just like I could when I was either bringing about life or trying to destroy it.

There it was—I could sense Prometheus.

I felt my body start to move through the water, as if some guiding force was drawing me to the island. I didn't know if it was me or someone on the island, but I continued to let it take me. A few moments later, I found myself on a beach, the sand sticking to my wet clothes.

No one was there, but I saw the cottage in the near distance. So that was all me. I never realized I could use my power to sense where energy was and call myself toward it. Perhaps it was a mix of my power and what I had absorbed from Prometheus.

Scrambling up, I ran toward the cottage. "Circe! Prometheus!"

Prometheus and Circe came running out of the cottage. I was still on the shore, trying to gather myself but realized that shifting to breathing underwater and breathing regular air was quite a challenge. I coughed up water and tried to take deep breaths, which only made it worse. Soon I was able to get it all out as Prometheus and Circe reached me.

"What happened?" He grabbed me by the shoulders. "What did you do?"

His eyes were dark, as if I had done the worst thing imaginable. Those were definitely not the eyes of a father. The sirens were more than likely telling the truth. It all made sense. I wanted to punch him or perhaps show him my power, but this wasn't the time.

But I could feel the darkness begin to swell once again. I held it back and took a deep breath.

"Sirens… they called me into the water. I couldn't do anything to stop myself."

He shook me. "I told you not to go into the water! Why didn't you listen?"

"I said, the sirens' song called me to it! I couldn't stop myself. I was under a trance!" More darkness gathered, and I saw as his hands jumped back. He must have felt it and realized his mistake.

Prometheus clenched his fist. "I knew I shouldn't have let you go out on your own. Damn it, Circe, I told you."

Circe slapped him in the back of his head. "Don't you dare drag me into this! I didn't realize sirens had been sent after her. I don't even know how their song was able to reach the island! This place is protected by my magic."

"Well, it isn't going to be anymore." He turned to me. "Now, tell me what happened."

"I… The sirens pulled me under, and then a god attacked us. One of the sirens got away and then… I killed Poseidon."

They just stared at me, as if they couldn't believe what I had said.

Prometheus let out a laugh. "I'm sorry, did you just say you killed Poseidon?"

I nodded slowly. "He was trying to kill me, and I had stop him." Tears started to fill my eyes when reality finally hit me. I had killed someone. I had killed a god. I didn't know who he was or anything. He had been trying to kill me without relent, yes, but that didn't mean he deserved to die. "He stabbed me with his trident, and two of the sirens died trying to protect me. I couldn't save them and I just— I used… some kind of dark power and drained his life source. There was no other way to escape."

Prometheus pulled me back up. "Right now is not the time for you to panic. Zeus is going to know where you are any minute now, and we have to figure out a way to get out of here and hide."

Circe shook her head. "No, he can't find this place. I made sure of it. He is the last person who would be able to find my island."

Turning to her, Prometheus explained, "A siren was able to pinpoint where she was, and one of them escaped Poseidon's attack. My bet is that the one survivor went and reported where we are and how to find us. It doesn't matter who she reported it to either. Zeus will be able to figure out that location and will be here any minute."

As if on cue, the once blue sky overhead started to darken with clouds. Prometheus looked up in horror, as did Circe. Apollo came running out of the cottage.

"What the hell is going on?" Apollo asked.

Prometheus took a deep breath. "Zeus has found out where we are. We don't have much time." He turned to Circe. "What do you think we should do?"

She stared up at the sky and shook her head. "There's no way we can leave without him noticing us. We will have to figure out a way to hide on the island."

Apollo was first to speak. "I have an idea. It might not work, but it's the best shot we've got."

"Well, speak!" Circe exclaimed. "We don't have time for your stupid mind games."

Apollo gave Circe a look but went on. "You used to turn humans into pigs and other animals, right? Can you do it to gods?"

I wrinkled my nose. Pigs? That was a bit barbaric. I watched as Circe pursed her lips.

"I did, once upon a time. But that was centuries ago. I'm not sure if those potions will even work anymore."

Prometheus shrugged. "It's our only option, is it not?"

Circe peered back up at the sky and then nodded. "Right, come with me. I think there are a few potions in my kitchen still."

We followed her inside as the sky grew darker and darker. I did not like the ominous feeling the energy brought. It was strong and powerful.

Was this Zeus? Was he able to control the sky like this? And if so, it contained so much energy that I didn't understand how he could think I was such a threat. It made me want to give up as I didn't believe there was any way I could fight against that kind of power.

But I didn't, as I still wanted to know the answers. I followed Circe and the others inside. Circe rushed to the kitchen and opened up cabinets, pulling out potion after potion. What were all those for? Why were there so many?

Then I noticed one labeled Lethe. I grabbed it and examined it further.

"This… this is what you bastards used on me!" I exclaimed, darkness starting to swirl around.

Prometheus's eyes widened. "Who told you— Never mind, this is not the time. Yes, I drugged you, but it was for your own good. I will explain later. Zeus will kill you. I never lied about that."

I held back the darkness and grabbed my head. "You have been using me. Everything was a lie."

"Not everything!" Prometheus exclaimed. "Now focus, we have to hide!"

I took deep breaths, knowing he was right. I would deal with him later. I stood back up and shot a look at Apollo as well. He turned away from me. Circe finally found the vials.

"Good, I still have three different ones left. Now, drink these, and don't say I didn't warn you. They are quite old."

I grabbed one of them and wondered if this would make me forget once again or if it would in fact turn me into an animal. I honestly didn't have anything to lose at that point. It was this or death.

Unscrewing the top, I downed the entire bottle. Never could I have imagined what would happen next.

CHAPTER 16

Huntley

It was so embarrassing to throw up after transporting. I had to make sure I didn't barf on Hades, as he wasn't in the best of moods. It explained why they never brought up this power before, as I would have been barfing all over them, but it also made sense that it left a sort of trail that Zeus could find. Now that Zeus was ahead of us, it didn't matter. Time was of the essence, and therefore I suffered.

Hades handed me some breath mints, and I was thankful he was prepared. I peered around and found that we were on a beach yet again. This time, however, there were no humans nearby. The sky was dark, and I knew Zeus was going to appear at any moment. I placed my hands over my eyes just as lightning struck the sand right in front of me. I wished I had simply shut them and put my hands over my ears instead as the deafening crash of thunder left my ears ringing for a good moment. Next time, I told myself, I would be smarter about it. I just hoped there wouldn't be a next time.

I stayed behind Hades, not wanting to get in the way if they started fighting again. A few moments later, another portal opened, and Persephone, Mel, Pothos, and AJ appeared. I wasn't quite sure why they brought AJ along as he didn't have his father to go report anything to anymore, but I didn't question it. Persephone probably didn't want him to run away as he still needed to atone for what he did.

As we all were now here, we turned to the one building that was close in the distance. It was a cottage, nestled between the trees. There was no movement from there, but I knew looks were deceiving.

But it definitely wasn't what I expected.

Zeus was the first to reach the front door of the cottage as we followed behind. I could tell Hades was on his guard for Chrys, as was I. He wasn't going to let Zeus get to her first.

The door opened to find a rather attractive woman dressed in a sort of bohemian look.

"Zeus. How the hell did you find this island?" she

asked in a rather surprised but calm manner.

He shook his head. "Don't play dumb with me. I am not in the forgiving mood. Tell me where she is right now!"

Circe glanced at all of us, still confused. "Who? No one but me lives on this island. Why are you all here?"

He shoved her out of the way and entered the cottage. Hades quickly followed. I was about to join him when I remembered all the times my father was mad at me and stormed into the apartment. I quickly went around the cottage to see if she was sneaking out the back.

I could still hear Zeus's thundering voice, no pun intended, as he kept asking Circe where she was hiding Chrys. So far it didn't sound like he found anything, which meant my hunch was probably correct.

Rounding to the back, I didn't find any trace of Chrys. She clearly wasn't anywhere near the cottage. I did, however, find a mutt that appeared to be a smaller lab mix. Maybe he was a border collie or something. I didn't know dogs that well. He was adorable, with black and white fur, and watched me closely as I searched for Chrys. He seemed interested in what I was doing but didn't leave the bones he was chewing on.

Something about him seemed odd, however. He kept his eyes on me like a good watch dog did, but they almost felt calculating and thinking. Then again, dogs were pretty smart.

"Huntley, did you find anything?" Persephone met up with me in the back.

I turned away from the dog and shook my head. "No, I don't see anything."

She frowned and then glanced at the dog and let out a breath. "Well that answers some things."

"What?"

Persephone shook her head. "Nothing. If she is here, we will be able to find her. Hopefully she is hiding good enough that Zeus will give up looking here and leave. Then we can find her ourselves."

So now the goal was to find her, convince Zeus she wasn't here, and then leave? I guess that made sense.

"Circe is a powerful witch, and she won't go down without a fight though. I just hope she will side with us in the end. I guess at least we know she won't side with Zeus." Persephone glanced at the dog. "As for the others, I'm not quite sure what they are going to end up doing."

She had a point. Prometheus and Apollo will have to choose a side. They wouldn't be able to go against both Hades and Zeus, and from what I knew about Prometheus, he was probably going to side with Hades. It was just a matter of whether Hades would forgive him for what he did.

Apollo, on the other hand, I had no idea what he would do. I didn't know him like I knew Prometheus,

although I guess in the end, I didn't really know
Prometheus all that well either. I had lived with him for
an entire year, and I still didn't expect him to commit
this kind of treachery. Well, maybe just a little.

He had it all planned out too and had deceived all of
us for a motive I still didn't quite grasp. I guess I
couldn't blame him—he wanted out from under Zeus's
thumb. I wanted Zeus gone as well, and I only had
known him for a year. But knowing how much the other
gods and lesser immortals despised him, I wasn't
surprised there were so many feuding plots to unseat
him from power.

I took another look around but didn't see any trace of
Chrys. As I started to go into the woods, I saw a little
black cat watching me. She was adorable, and I wanted
to go cuddle her but decided not to. I had learned my
lesson in trying to pick up a cat who didn't know me,
and I had the scars to prove it.

Not wanting to get lost in these woods, I headed back
to the cottage to see if Hades or Persephone found
anything. As I got closer, I heard both Zeus and Hades
yelling. Great, another fight was going to break out.

"Circe, I know she is here! Why else would you have
two extra bedrooms full of clothes for two men and a
woman? You don't live with anyone else!" Zeus
screamed at her.

I could feel some dark energy coming off Circe.

Persephone wasn't kidding; she did have a lot of power. "Sometimes a couple of humans visit for sex! Is that so wrong? I am alone after all!"

Pothos and Mel stayed way back from the fight that was erupting, and Mel kept AJ at her side. They knew as well as I that we were all just witnesses and couldn't do anything to stop what was about to happen.

"Yeah right! You and I both know that no one comes here anymore! Not since Odysseus."

"If no one comes here, then how would Prometheus know where I am?" Circe growled.

Hades started yelling. "We know she's here! Just tell us where she is! I don't want to cause problems. I just want my daughter back!"

"She isn't here! Leave before I snap!" Circe yelled back.

I had to give it to her, she was pretty strong-willed if she was willing to argue with these two gods.

Zeus shook his head. "Do you not understand? Poseidon is dead! My brother is dead! You think I am going to simply back down?"

"I'm sorry for your loss, Zeus, but as you can see, she isn't here! I'm not hiding her so just leave me out of this!" She gestured at the gray sky that threatened to erupt in rain. "Can you see why I don't let any of you gods on my island? Because I don't want to get involved in all your shit!"

"Circe, my daughter is missing. Please, tell me where she is." Hades tried to take a calmer approach, which I honestly didn't think would ever work.

"Sorry, Hades, but I have no idea where your daughter is. I wouldn't have gotten involved in such a messy situation, and you all know that. Now leave!"

Zeus took a deep breath and let it out slowly. "Fine, you all leave me with no choice."

He turned to me, and I could feel my fight-or-flight instincts kick in, mainly the flight one. I turned to start running, but there was no use. Zeus grabbed me by the back of the neck in an instant, and a knife suddenly appeared in his other hand.

"Oh, Chrys! Come out, come out, wherever you are! I have your precious human husband, and I will kill him if you don't come out!"

Shit, this wasn't going to end well. I was now a liability. I was weak—I should have stayed away. I tried to struggle, but Zeus was much stronger than I was. He held the knife under my throat. I gulped as the blade was right against the skin. I couldn't move. I couldn't do anything.

"Chrys, I don't have time for you to try to call my bluff. I give you five seconds to come out!" His voice, I could feel, traveled across the island. "Five!"

There was nothing. No sound as no one tried to stop him, not even Hades.

"Four."

I wanted her to come out, but I didn't want her to risk her life.

"Three."

I closed my eyes. This was going to be the end. I was going to die. Again.

"Two!"

Shit. Shit. Shit.

"One!"

I felt as he began to press the knife against my throat.

"Wait!" I heard Chrys scream.

I opened my eyes to see the cat transforming in front of me. She appeared as beautiful as she ever did, but the way she looked at me was different. She appeared confused as her eyebrows furrowed and she hesitated.

"Who... who is this human and why does my chest hurt?" she asked.

CHAPTER 17

Chrys

"Why do I feel I need to help you? Why does my heart ache seeing you in trouble?" I asked as I transformed back into human form. I felt that this was probably the stupidest decision I would ever make, but something about seeing this boy in trouble... I knew I couldn't let it happen.

Zeus smiled. "Well, there she is. The girl of the hour."

"Let him go."

Zeus raised an eyebrow. "You say you don't remember him, and yet you risk your life to save him?"

"I know he means something to me, and it's the first thing I have felt to be true in the past few days. So let him go!" I yelled. I knew he was important to me. Was he my friend? Someone I loved? That had to be it—it was the only reason my heart would hurt so much seeing him in danger.

Zeus laughed. "Why would I care if you want him freed or not? You will be meeting your fate soon enough. Speaking of which…" He glanced around. "Where are the other two? Are they hiding as animals as well? Prometheus, Apollo, come out, come out wherever you are!" Zeus had a little smile on his lips, but I could tell that he was mostly satisfied that he had found me. Apollo and Prometheus could wait to be dealt with.

I glanced back and saw Apollo in his dog form, but I had no idea where Prometheus would hide while in his bird form. Perhaps he was long gone. I wouldn't blame him—his plan had failed, and he was about to meet the wrath of Zeus. If I were him, I would have run too. I wanted to hide, but seeing this human almost die—I couldn't just watch.

Zeus turned a little to Circe. "See, I was right. You were hiding them."

She rolled her eyes but didn't say anything. I felt a little bad that she had been caught up in this mess, but then I realized it was her own fault. They had lied to me.

Looking back to me, Zeus went on. "But as for you,

Chrys, you are going to die right here and now."

Hades stepped in front of me. Seeing him brought me some kind of comfort, but I still wasn't sure why. Could he truly be my father?

"You are not killing my daughter!" Hades demanded.

"Hades, we have been over this! She has to die. She can't be allowed to have all the power she possesses!"

"But I can take her to the Underworld and lock her away for the rest of eternity, just don't send her to Tartarus! She doesn't deserve that kind of punishment!" Hades exclaimed.

He was risking his life for me. Was he truly my father? I didn't see Prometheus anywhere near us, meanwhile this god was willing to risk everything. So it had to be true. This man was, in fact, my father.

I was the daughter of Hades—the daughter of the Underworld.

Zeus went on. "She can revive herself if she was in any place except Tartarus! I will not allow it! I will not allow another god to be revived or killed like she has done!"

This conversation was truly going nowhere, and Zeus still held that human in his arms. The knife was barely touching his neck, and I could see blood starting to trickle down his throat.

He was going to kill him at any moment. I had to do something.

I was still far from Zeus, so if I tried to get closer, he would have time to kill the human. My power of death wasn't very exact, and it killed everything in the surrounding area. There was no way I would be able to focus it just on Zeus, especially with the human so close.

Which left only one thing to do.

I took a deep breath and asked the spirit of the vegetation around me to surround Zeus and grab him. I knew Zeus would easily break away from it, but it would be enough time for me to grab the human and get him out of there. Then I could attack Zeus full force.

Well, maybe. My power did go every which way. If it got out of control, I could probably destroy the whole island. I had already done a number on the ocean floor.

I reached out to the plants, and they responded exactly how I needed them to. Vines reached out and grabbed Zeus by the wrist, causing him to drop the knife he was holding.

While he was distracted, I quickly ran and grabbed the human, shoving him forward toward the other people that he had traveled with. A woman caught him and pulled him aside. That was finished—now I could fight without worrying about casualties. Hopefully.

Zeus laughed. "You have become more powerful, I see. And what, after just a couple of days? Hades, you wonder why I must destroy her? It's because she can master such power so quickly."

"If you want to kill her, you will have to destroy me first! I will not go on living if my own daughter is in Tartarus."

Zeus pulled one of his arms free from the vine. "So be it!"

A large bolt of lightning came piercing down from the sky, nearly blinding me. I was thrown back from the force and watched as Zeus directed it straight at Hades.

"No!" I screamed.

To my surprise, it didn't seem that Hades got much of the hit but was able to block it with his own powers. His power, I felt, was a lot like half of mine. Darkness spilled out from every direction. The only difference was that he could control it and it wasn't instant death like mine. No, this felt like shadows and damage, but it didn't affect the energy of a living thing around it like mine did.

Maybe I was too powerful. If the god of the Underworld couldn't even affect the life force of something, why could I?

"Chrys, run!" Hades yelled. "Get out of here!"

My feet felt as if they couldn't move in all of this— there was too much going on. I felt like collapsing, but instead I ran straight at Zeus, calling up my own power. I could destroy him just like I did Poseidon, and then I wouldn't have to worry about anything ever again. I wouldn't cause anyone any more trouble.

I gathered as much of the energy as I could and began to direct it straight at Zeus.

Just as I was about to let it go, I felt something grab my shoulders and lift me up.

"What the—?"

I peered up to find Prometheus's altered form carrying me away from the island. Even though he wasn't actually an eagle, I was surprised he could hold up my weight.

"Prometheus, let me go!" I screamed, watching as he flew over the ocean. I needed to get back there—I needed to destroy Zeus.

"You aren't powerful enough! He will kill you! Let Hades weaken him and then you will be able to attack!"

"Hades? You mean my father, you lying son of a bitch!"

He didn't say anything as he kept on flying. I could feel my power want to go out of control—especially since I had already drawn so much of it forward already. I took a deep breath and let it go back inside, deep into my heart. I had to forgive Prometheus for the time being, as I didn't want to drop down into the middle of the water.

As I looked back, I found we had another problem. The dark sky was following us, and lightning strikes began to lash out all around us.

"Are you sure we are going to be fine up here?" I exclaimed.

"We have no choice. I think if we move fast enough, we can beat him!"

I wasn't too sure about that as more and more lightning emitted from the sky. It crashed around us, and I could smell the ozone. I watched as it got closer and closer. If one of those bolts hit us, I doubted we would be able to survive. Something seemed different about them compared to the normal, natural lightning strikes. These seemed to have a power that could send someone down into the depths of Tartarus.

Parts of the Underworld were coming back to me. I remembered being there, although the details were still sketchy. Tartarus was the land of the damned—a pit that extended on forever. It was somewhere one could never escape. It was somewhere I didn't want to go.

The lightning followed us to wherever Prometheus was taking us. He dodged as lightning struck into the water again and again. I had to hand it to him—he was quite good at flying.

"Where are we going?" I called up to him.

"The closest city is Athens. There we can make our escape."

"You think I would want to go anywhere with you?"

"No, once we are on land, you can make a run for it, and I will be going the opposite way."

I shook my head. "Nice, so I am bait while you can escape. Thanks."

"I know that I would be able to hide this time. If Zeus wins, he will come after me and deal my punishment, and if you win, I doubt you won't hold a grudge."

"Then why did you do all this? Did you even expect to ever win?"

"I just wanted Zeus destroyed. I was overzealous about the idea of it and didn't think he would find us this fast. I had hoped that you would forgive me and I could help you rule Olympus. If it weren't for Persephone, we would have gotten a lot further in all this."

I let out a sigh. "I knew you were lying to me. I overheard you talking to Apollo the other night and how you never wanted me to find my memories. But also, I don't want to rule Olympus—I just want to survive."

Prometheus was silent and kept flying toward what appeared to be a city. Was this Athens? Was it somewhere I had been before?

"When we land, I want you to run and keep running. Don't look back. Maybe you are right and you can defeat Zeus, or maybe your father will find you and succeed in protecting you this time. Whatever it may be, just keep running. I wish you all the luck."

My feet touched down on the ground, and I began to

run as people stared at me, confused why an eagle had carried me.

But I didn't look back.

CHAPTER 18

Huntley

Well, none of us saw that coming.

A giant eagle had grabbed Chrys and flew off faster than any of us could respond. Even Zeus was too slow to break himself free and do anything about it, not to mention Hades was standing in his way. He probably figured it was the best way to keep his daughter safe for the time being.

It was probably Prometheus who grabbed her, and now he was taking her somewhere to hide once again. Did this guy never give up?

Prometheus had erased her memories and was using her for his own gain. Granted, everyone wanted to see Zeus destroyed for one reason or another, but to use someone innocent was not forgivable. She had suffered so much at all these gods' hands—I just wanted all of us to return to the Underworld and forget any of this ever happened. But that wasn't going to happen. No, we were far from that.

It started to hit me—she didn't remember who I was.

She tried to save me even though she didn't know who I was. She had said that her heart told her that we were close but couldn't think of any of the reasons why or recall our history together. Half of me couldn't believe it was true and worried that she would never regain memories of our time together, but the other half was happy that our love was powerful enough to endure.

I tried not to think about the fact that she may never remember and that I could lose that part of her. Even if she didn't recognize me though, I would never leave her side. I knew she would do the same for me.

Zeus broke free from the vines and ivy that wrapped his arms. "Let me through, Hades! Prometheus just ran off with your daughter!"

"Better him than you!" Hades snarled.

Zeus raised his hand, and lightning began to spread out through the waters. I watched in horror as Prometheus flew around it all, careful not to get hit. He was like a sitting duck out there—Prometheus better know what he was doing.

Hades tackled Zeus. Like, actually full on tackled him. I didn't think he would have such rough combat skills in him. I watched as the eagle that carried Chrys got farther away. Hades' plan worked—he was able to distract Zeus long enough so they could get away from the lightning.

Zeus rolled over and punched Hades square in the jaw. "Stop helping Prometheus!"

Hades threw a punch back. "I'm not! I'm helping my daughter!"

They rolled on the ground, throwing punches like some high school fight. It brought back memories of all the times I fought, but this was definitely a fight I wasn't going to get in the middle of. But I could tell they were brothers.

I backed away and stood over next to Pothos and Mel. I leaned in toward Pothos so no one else could hear. "So, like, this is a weird brawl right?"

He nodded. "Yeah, usually it's not like this—usually they fight with their powers. It's kind of entertaining though. Never would I have imagined Hades getting down in the dirt like this."

I held back a laugh, as I didn't want to die that day. Mel watched, confused as well. Persephone moved over toward us.

"Men will always be boys, I swear."

Mel nodded. "But at least it is giving Chrys some

time to get out of here."

Persephone nodded. "Right, of which we need to head out and find her. Knowing Prometheus, he will probably throw her in the middle of a city to run and hide. We have to find her first and get her to the Underworld before those two finally stop brawling."

"What's the closest city?" I asked.

"Athens," Persephone explained. "And Huntley, please don't throw up on me."

I nodded with a sigh. I hated transporting so much. Placing my hand on Persephone's shoulder, we were transported into a city. We were probably only moments before Zeus would follow. We had to find her fast.

But first I had to throw up. I turned and vomited on the street. Luckily, I didn't get it on anyone, but I did make Mel jump back five feet, dragging AJ along with her. I was surprised he wasn't trying to run at that point, although I had a feeling it was because he knew there was no use.

"That's disgusting, Huntley!" Mel yelled. "You almost puked on me!"

I bent over, not sure if more was going to come up. "Sorry, I was focusing on not throwing up on Persephone."

Persephone patted my back. "Oh, Huntley, I'm sorry you get sick. Hopefully this will be the last time."

I nodded. "Yeah, me too."

Once I could stand up without feeling nauseated, I popped a breath mint in my mouth from the pack that Hades had given me earlier. "Okay, what should we do now?"

"Split up," Pothos said. "Try to cover as much ground to find them."

"We can stay in contact with our cell phones," Mel explained. "If any of us find Chrys or Prometheus, we can grab them and hide until Persephone can get to that person and head to the Underworld."

"That sounds good to me," I said. "Let's go."

We all started heading out in different directions. I had never been to Athens before, obviously, and it was strange to see a Greek temple on a hill in the middle of this massive city. Having been in London, I was starting to get used to the mix of new and old architecture, but this temple was even older than any architecture in London. It was just so surreal and strange to witness this.

I had to focus. I had to find Chrys.

Glancing around, I didn't even know where to start. If I were her and she had gotten away from Prometheus, I would just start running as far from the city, knowing that people would be looking for me in specific hiding spots.

So she probably was trying to get out to the countryside and stay low.

However, I had no idea which way that would be. I thought about asking someone but realized I didn't speak Greek. I didn't know who would speak English, and I didn't want to seem like some stupid tourist.

But then again, Chrys's life was on the line.

I stopped a young guy on the street, appearing about my age before I died. "Which way is the edge of the city?"

He looked at me strangely and then pointed in a direction.

I nodded. "Thanks!"

It didn't help that all the signs were written with Greek letters, as it made me even more confused. If it were written with roman letters, at least I could pick out maybe a few words. Maybe.

I ran down the streets, keeping my eyes open for Chrys' beautiful hair in the crowded streets. There were so many tourists that I didn't even know where to start. It was as bad as London. I wondered how far she could have gotten and whether Persephone was correct about her being there. There were only four of us scouting this entire city, and she could be anywhere.

I just hoped I would find her first.

Suddenly it sounded like the world was ending.

Looking up at the sky, I found clouds rolling in more quickly than what a scientist would deem possible, and lightning began to terrorize the area when only moments before it had been sunny and warm.

Zeus was here.

Dark energy also exploded in the sky, and I was glad to see that Hades was also here. It seems their battle was not over, which was lucky for us in a way. He would distract Zeus while we found Chrys, or at least tried. I just hoped that he would survive long enough to see his daughter again.

All the people in the streets hurried inside as rain began to pour down. My clothes soaked quickly, but I didn't care. It wasn't like I could get sick any longer, and the cold never bothered me growing up. Having lived in a junky trailer and sometimes out on the street, I was used to it. Besides, I would run through a blizzard if it meant saving Chrys. No rain was going to stop me.

The buildings began to space themselves out more, and I knew that I was about at the edge of the city. The storm was a lot less severe out here, and I was able to see a lot better. Glancing back, I found Hades and Zeus in the sky, fighting. I wondered how much of this was going to end up on YouTube. Probably most of it by hundreds of different users as I saw a few people out in the streets with their phones, taking videos. If the gods ever wanted more people to believe in them, here was their chance.

Turning my eyes back to the road in front of me, I saw a girl running as fast as I was. Her hair was soaked, but I would have recognized it anywhere—it was Chrys.

"Chrys!" I yelled. "Wait!"

She turned her head, and I could tell she didn't know if she should slow down or not. She still didn't remember me, but she risked her life to save me.

"Please, I just want to help!" I yelled.

Chrys slowed down a little, and I pulled her into an alleyway so no one could see us, including the gods up in the sky.

"Chrys, it's okay, I'm here."

She was shivering, and I wasn't sure if it was from the rain or everything that was going on. I wrapped my arms around her, and she began to cry.

"I don't know what's right or wrong, who is telling the truth and who is lying to me," she sobbed. "Who are you? How long have we known each other? Why can't I remember?"

I stroked her back. "Shh, we will figure out how to get your memories back. For now, I can tell you that we have known each other for a few years now and... I love you with everything I have. I would do anything for you."

She was quiet for a moment and then pulled back enough to look me in the eyes. "I can feel I love you too, but I don't know why."

I kissed her and pulled her close. She didn't resist.

"Huntley…?" she said as she remembered my name. Suddenly pain was apparent on her face and she grabbed her head. "Ow…"

"What's wrong?" I asked, although a little excited she remembered my name.

"Anytime I remember something, my head starts to pound."

That must have been because of the drug Prometheus had given her. "Okay, stop trying to remember for now —we have to get out of here."

She shook her head. "There is no use. They will find us eventually."

I grabbed her hand and kissed her knuckles. "No, I won't allow it. We have come too far for it all to end like this. I will make sure you are fine, and I won't let anyone take you away from me."

Chrys slowly nodded. "Okay, I trust you."

I smiled and then grabbed my phone. "I'll call your mom. She will be able to get us into the Underworld where Zeus won't be able to touch you."

As I went for my phone, she grabbed my hand. "Wait, I still don't know who to trust. Are you sure?"

"Yes. She would do anything for you."

"But what if Zeus sees her coming this way? Then he will know where we are."

She did have a point. If I alert the others and Zeus sees all of them going to this location, he is going to be able to tell where we are. I had a feeling, though, Persephone was smarter than that and would figure out a way to find us, grab Chrys, and take her to the Underworld.

At least I hoped.

"I think it will be okay. Your mom is smart."

She nodded and I quickly texted her our location. In an instant, Persephone was standing before us.

Persephone grabbed Chrys's wrist. "We don't have much time. We have to get you to the Underworld. Huntley, you might barf."

"That's fine. Let's just get out of here."

And with that, Persephone transported us to the entrance of the Underworld.

CHAPTER 19

Chrys

Persephone, who was said to be my mother, transported us to a world that I had started to remember. It was dark and yet everything around me glowed blue. It made me feel happy and at ease, but I wasn't exactly sure why. I could sense death around me, but it wasn't the death that marked the end, but a new beginning.

This was the Underworld. This was my home.

Huntley turned and started vomiting away from Persephone and me. I wondered why he did that and I felt fine. By the looks of it, Persephone was also fine. Was it because he was a human and gods felt fine transporting like this? Was I capable of also transporting? If I was, I wish I had known earlier as then I could have gotten away from everything and hidden until I felt safe enough to leave.

Persephone kept her grip on my wrist, and I didn't budge. I felt safer around her than I had with any other god or creature thus far, besides the human Huntley. Perhaps she was my mother.

"We have to hurry and get into the Underworld before Zeus figures out where we are. Once we are inside, Zeus can't follow and we will be able to hide you until all this blows over."

I nodded, feeling a little warmth in my heart from this woman. I could tell she meant something to me, even if the feelings were a bit complicated. I followed her as she led us to a man standing at a boat.

I wondered how long this would actually take to blow over. Zeus seemed to be pretty persistent and keen on destroying me, so I doubt I would be out of the clear anytime soon. I didn't want to kill another person like I had Poseidon. It didn't feel right even if it was in self-defense.

But what else was I supposed to do?

As we hurried to the entrance, something came flying down from above. We all stopped as the man landed in front of me. He looked at me with such sad blue eyes. His brown hair was ruffled and his face a bit scruffy, as if he hadn't been sleeping and didn't know what he was about to do next.

The interesting part was that he felt familiar, as if we had a bond, but by the look on his face, I felt whatever bond we had was going to be broken soon.

"Hermes." Persephone shook her head. "You can't be serious. You are the one who helped us in the first place. Now you are turning your back on us?"

Hermes let out a tired sigh. "My hands are tied, Persephone. Zeus knew you would try to make a run for it to the Underworld. If I don't obey him, he will kill me."

"So you are willing to kill my child? There is no way —I won't stand for this!" My mother let me go, and I could feel energy gathering around her—the same energy I used to bring the plants back to life.

"Chrys, run for the ferry! Charon will take you down to the Underworld! I will deal with Hermes!"

Huntley grabbed me and we started for the ferry. Hermes tried to reach for me, but vines came shooting out of the ground and bound his arms and legs. By the look on Hermes's face, he was surprised she could do such a thing down here in the entrance of the Underworld. Even I was having a hard time finding energy I could harness. She had done it in one smooth swoop. My mother was a badass.

Hermes let out a sigh as he tried to get out of the vines. They wouldn't budge. "Persephone, please, let's be reasonable."

Huntley and I pushed forward toward the ferry where a man stood on a boat, ready to take us. I felt like I should help, but I didn't know what to do next. I needed to get out of there, then try to regain my memories. All of this was so confusing and I couldn't believe just days before I thought I was someone else's daughter. Now I found out I was actually the daughter of the god of the Underworld, and I was supposed to never have been born.

My head started to ache even worse now, causing me to not focus on where I was stepping and trip. I hit the ground hard, as most of what surrounded us were hard rocks with no vegetation to speak of, other than the vines my mother had summoned.

Huntley reached down to try to help, but I pushed him back as I felt more of the dark energy begin to pour out of me. It would kill him, and I didn't want to let that happen.

"Get away from me!"

He looked down at me in shock, but the next thing I knew, the darkness engulfed me, lashing out every which way. I tried to take a deep breath and stay calm, but there was no use. I had to get out of there, or I would destroy everyone around me.

Doing the only thing that seemed reasonable, I ignored the ferry and the god in the boat who waved at me as if I were some friend and jumped in the strange blue liquid that made up the water. I let it consume me like the ocean did, but this liquid felt different. It was cold, but in its essence rather than its temperature. It felt like death in physical form.

I didn't know if I could get down to the Underworld without using the ferry, but I was willing to give it a shot so that nothing around me was destroyed. Being down in the liquid, maybe the dark energy that consumed me would slow down and not take form. Now that I felt a bit more safe, I started swimming forward to figure out what I was going to do next and how I was going to get away from there.

As I began to swim farther from the area where the boat had been, I noticed the current was getting stronger and stronger. I tried to swim with it but keep my control. At first all was fine, and I could keep my body from rolling around, but the farther I went, the less I could move. Suddenly the current was in complete control and I was thrashing about.

That was a big mistake.

I couldn't make out which way was up or down. The current seemed to go be haphazardous, and soon I felt as many currents began to pull me toward them. The river apparently was splitting, and I had to leave it up to fate for which one would take me and just pray that it was the right choice.

Fate took me down one of the rivers, and the feeling

of the water began to change. It felt almost sticky and putrid. I opened my mouth and tasted something familiar. It tasted of rotting flesh, which shouldn't have been something familiar. It was disgusting and foul, but it reminded me of something—a memory.

My mind was screaming now. I knew what this was —it was the liquid that Prometheus used to take away my memories. The more it consumed me, the more all those memories started to come back to me. How it was possible, I had no idea. All I knew was that the more I struggled, the more I breathed in, the more I somehow could remember everything before losing my memories.

I was the daughter of Hades and Persephone.

I had lived in the Underworld all my life. Recently I went to the mortal realm to see why my mother loved it more. I was discovered by both Poseidon and Zeus, putting me in a position where I'd have to marry Zeus. Then I found out I was already married to Huntlcy, and the wedding was fortunately called off. Poseidon tried to convince Zeus I was going to betray them, leaving Zeus to declare war on me.

And then Prometheus made me take the vial of Lethe and I forgot everything. He tried to make me kill Zeus, although that wasn't looking too bad currently. Killing Zeus might be the only way to stop all of this.

As I recalled everything, I felt something grab me

and pull me up out of the water. I gasped for air, and as I adjusted my eyes, I saw that it was Hermes. I knew who he was now, and I knew all he had done for me over the past few months.

"Hermes? But… why?" I asked. He had been like a friend and had saved me multiple times. Yet now he had turned his back on me and was helping Zeus. The smiling face and mischievous demeanor were now gone and replaced with sorrow.

"I… I can't disobey him. You understand, don't you? This is the end of everything, and I have to think of my own life."

I did understand. If he went against Zeus again, Zeus would simply send him to Tartarus. I couldn't blame Hermes, as I was just trying to save my own life too. And I had killed Poseidon, so I had the power to do it.

But could I kill Hermes to stop him from taking me back to Earth? I looked deep into those blue eyes that belonged to a person I learned to trust and consider a friend—the eyes that joked with me and played pranks with me. Could I kill him to save my own skin?

I felt darkness begin to form at my hands as he started flying up to Oceanus. The darkness dissipated as my heart took over the power. No, I couldn't—I couldn't hurt him on purpose. Now that my memories were back, I felt as if I had a little more control over everything. If I wanted to kill him, I would have to do it deliberately right now.

But I couldn't kill him. Not after everything.

He would take me to Zeus, and I could face him once and for all. If I destroyed Zeus, I wouldn't have to run anymore. I could be free and so could many other gods. It was the only way to stop this.

I just prayed that I had enough strength.

CHAPTER 20

Huntley

And there she went.

I couldn't believe Chrys just leaped into the water and totally ignored the ferry. I mean, I knew why as I felt the power coming off her as she freaked out. Something must have spooked her, or she started to remember some things. Either way though, now it was going to be a pain to try to find her.

"Son of a bitch!" I yelled as I ran to the water and looked all around. I couldn't see anything. The water was either too dark or the current had already swept her away. Perhaps it was both.

From what I knew, people weren't supposed to swim in the water. Those who did were lost souls, and it took a long time for them all to be found by Charon. At least since we knew she was out there, we would be able to find her. I didn't know how vast the rivers truly were though. Hopefully we located her quickly, or she could get out of it on her own.

Turning back to where Persephone and Hermes were, I watched in amazement as Persephone called upon the power of nature as she fought Hermes. I knew she was the goddess of nature and all that, but I had never actually seen her fight. It was quite awesome, actually. I didn't know she had it in her.

What was interesting, and what I was confused about, was how easily Hermes could get out of the vines now. Just moments ago he acted like he couldn't leave them and let Chrys and I run. Was he hoping we would get away? Was he giving Chrys a chance so it would appear as if he did his duty for Zeus?

The man didn't make sense, but I wasn't going to question it any longer.

Hermes slipped out of the grasp of the vines, as if he were some kind of magician doing a magic trick. He could totally do some kind of performance for humans and amaze them. I wondered how many gods did use their powers to earn some money.

I shook my head. Now was not the time.

Persephone summoned vine after vine, some that looked like ivy, some that were covered in thorns. I could tell she was using any plant she could think of to wrap him up and stop him, but nothing was working. He could pass through anything, although some of the thorns did scratch his clothes.

I stood there like an idiot, not sure what to do. There was no way I could stop Hermes. I had to admit, his betrayal hurt a bit as he seemed like a pretty cool guy. I wanted to know more about him, but it appeared he was just another one of Zeus's lackeys.

"Hermes, I swear, if you hurt my daughter, I will never forgive you! I will make you pay! Hades will make you pay! Our wrath is nothing compared to Zeus!"

"Persephone, I'm sorry, but you know I have to take her to Zeus. I can't disobey him again. He can send me to Tartarus."

I wished I could help, but at that point, there was nothing I could do but watch. I didn't have the power to go after Chrys, and I didn't have the power to fight Hermes. I just had to sit there and wait, hoping that Persephone could somehow handle Hermes on her own.

What was I thinking? I was a punk—there was always some way I could get in the middle of a fight. I glanced around. I couldn't exactly tackle Hermes since he was up in the air now, but I could distract him with something.

I had learned that there were a few ways to distract

someone during a fight, besides tackling them. First was to throw something at them, second was to blind them with a mirror of some sort, and third was to use a loud sound. I, of course, had none of those things currently.

But maybe someone did.

Turning to Charon, I asked. "Do you have a mirror?"

He nodded and pulled one out. "I always keep one in case I get a hot chick I have to transport to the Underworld and I want to make sure I look my best. There was this one time—"

"Thanks." I grabbed it before he could go on with the story. Knowing him, it would take forever for him to tell his whole account, and the battle would be long over.

Except I realized I didn't have any light. The sun didn't exist down here—it was all just shimmering blue darkness.

"Shit."

I turned back to Charon, who was still muttering the story under his breath. I gave him a smile. "Charon… do you have a laser pointer by chance?"

He pulled it out. "Funny story…"

I grabbed it and handed him back the mirror. I pointed the laser straight at Hermes's eyes, hoping it would work. Don't try this at home kids.

It worked. He flinched as it burned him right in the

eyes and used his hands to try to block it, leaving him open for Persephone to attack. She noticed his lack of concentration and summoned all her vines to tie around his body. Before he could use his magic to get out of the hold, she smacked him on the ground. He hit the rocks with a loud thud and didn't move. She had knocked him out cold.

Persephone turned to me and let out a breath. "Thank you."

I shrugged. "No biggie."

"Now, help me get him on the ferry while we go look for Chrys. I don't want to let him out of my sight."

I nodded and helped her lug Hermes over to Charon's boat. He simply watched and didn't offer to help.

"Well, this will be a first—Hermes going into the Underworld in my boat. Crazy, he always sneaks in on his own. I haven't ever figured it out how he does it though. Maybe when he wakes I can ask him."

Persephone held back a snappy comment. "Just get going, Charon. We have to find Chrys."

"Right! It was strange to see her simply leap into the water. She didn't really think it through, now did she? The current will sweep her away," Charon said as he began moving the boat through the water. "Only master ferrymen like myself are able to navigate such treacherous waters."

I couldn't believe he didn't seem to notice that there

was practically a battle going on and Chrys had been running away for her life. Was he really so oblivious?

"So, as I was saying about the mirror," Charon went on. I rolled my eyes. "There was the beautiful woman, I believe her name was Marilyn, and she came to my boat and I couldn't believe it. She was so nice too. A sweetheart. But I checked my mirror, and I had ketchup all over my face! I looked like such a slob." He laughed. "Oh, it was so funny. She helped clean me up, but I was so embarrassed. I mean, I had already delivered so many people since lunch, and none of them had said a thing!"

I glanced over to Persephone. She shrugged. It couldn't be helped, I supposed, as Charon never shut up.

Persephone and I went to the opposite sides of the boat and scanned the waters for Chrys. Charon kept talking, but I wasn't listening. I was too focused on finding Chrys. I couldn't let anything more happen to her. She already had been through so much. I just wanted to take her, wrap her up in a blanket, and not let anything else ever hurt her again.

Except I was a human and there was little I could do against these gods.

Letting out a sigh, I kept scanning the waters for something—anything—but I only saw water everywhere.

Then, in the distance, I saw something in the water. I pointed. "Charon, head that way!"

"The River Lethe. All right, just make sure you don't touch the water as it can erase memories."

Yes, we knew that. But if she was in that river, would she forget everything that had happened again? Would we be back at where we started? I didn't even want to think what that would entail. I just knew we had to hurry before she was even worse off.

Charon steered the boat toward the river, and I could see that she was struggling against the current. I wanted to tell Charon to hurry it up, but I knew that wouldn't get us anywhere. We were almost within reach now when I heard a splash of water. I turned to find Hermes had disappeared and Persephone's eyes were wide.

Hermes had jumped into the water after Chrys.

"Shit!" I said as I carefully peered over the side of the boat. Persephone did the same.

"Well. Hermes is a goner," Charon commented. "No one can withstand that liquid."

Persephone shook her head. "You are wrong for two reasons, Charon. First off, Hermes can go through anything, so he isn't actually touching the water and will be okay. And second, there was someone who had used the poison in the river and succeeded in becoming powerful as a result."

"Oh yeah. Him. I didn't like him."

"Who?" I asked.

Persephone answered. "Hercules. He was able to use the herb henbane, which is connected to Lethe, to become stronger and navigate the Underworld. He was the only demigod to ever do such a thing, however."

Suddenly Hermes came shooting out of the water with Chrys in his arms. He kept flying higher and higher, heading back into the mortal realm.

Persephone turned to Charon. "Head back to the entrance. We need to alert Hades before it is too late!"

Charon nodded and started to turn the boat back around. "This is the most excitement I have had in a long while. In fact, I think the last time was—"

I interrupted his story. "Why don't we transport from here? Or message him on our phone?"

Persephone explained, "Because, no one can transport into the Underworld except to the entrance, and I have found that cell phones don't work down here."

It made sense. Unfortunately.

Persephone sighed. "But by the look of Chrys, it seems she is okay. In fact…"

"What?" I asked.

"I think it's possible that drowning in that river has restored her memories. Her face was different—like it understood now, and she wasn't struggling against Hermes. The power of the River Lethe all depends on who possesses it. Yes, it is used to forget your memories, but it is also used to strengthen your mental power. Since she wanted to know more, I think the Lethe granted her that wish. Hecate blessed this river using her herb henbane. It is a poison that can make you forget everything, which is why we typically give it to humans when they go to the afterlife. That way they are happy and can enjoy themselves without remembering anything that happened on Earth. But as I said earlier, Hercules used the plant to strengthen his power and journey through the Underworld without being harmed."

I looked up at Hermes and Chrys. So it was possible she remembered now. I couldn't believe that this was how she regained her memories, but I was happy that it was possible. Now we just needed to get back and finish this once and for all.

CHAPTER 21

Chrys

This wasn't happening.

I stared down at Athens, watching as my father and Zeus battled it out. There were fires erupting now throughout the city as they made their way toward the Acropolis. Citizens and tourists were frantically running through the streets, confused, and trying to get away from whatever disaster was happening but also had their phones out, taking videos of what was going on. The sky was dark with thunderclouds and what one would only describe as death. I had never seen my father use his powers at full strength like that. They were using their powers at such a force that it didn't appear that even helicopters could get up in the sky.

My father must have not wanted to make a scene in London before Zeus defeated him, as he didn't wield power like that during that battle, as I would have felt it. This power, however, was so thick that I could barely breath, if it weren't for the fact that I was a goddess of darkness as well.

I never thought I would be afraid of what power my father had until that moment.

As I looked down at the battlefield, I realized I had lost my chance of getting away. There was no way now that I would be able to win against Zeus. I should have fought Hermes down in the Underworld where I had the advantage. Now I was just screwed.

"I'm sorry," Hermes whispered. "I wish things could have ended up differently."

I nodded. "Yeah, me too."

"If I could have done anything, I would have. But at this point, my hands are tied. If I don't help Zeus, he will torture me for an eternity."

I turned to him to find tears running down his face. I smiled a little, glad that he cared enough to feel something. "Thank you. You tried to help Huntley, and if it weren't for Poseidon and AJ, none of this would have happened. We were almost in the clear just days ago, but Poseidon tricked us all."

"And Prometheus."

I nodded. "Yes, him too."

"And Apollo," Hermes added.

"And all the gods really. It doesn't seem any are on my side."

"Not as long as Zeus is alive, no. But I don't think anyone would try to stop you if you tried killing him."

I shook my head. "There is no way that I could kill him. He's too strong."

"You killed Poseidon."

He had a point. It wasn't even that hard, and we were underwater, which was in his domain. "He's not as strong as the god of gods."

"I think if you keep telling yourself you can't, then you will fail, but if you weren't a threat to him, then he wouldn't care whether you were alive."

If I wasn't powerful enough to take him down, then he wouldn't be trying so hard to kill me. I had turned everything around in the past year—more than I could ever imagine.

I guess I might as well go out with a bang rather than just accept my inevitable death.

"I have felt your power when you almost fell into Tartarus. It was wild and out of control, so I didn't get the full blow, but don't doubt it. It is something that can destroy any life, even Zeus's. Don't tell him I said this, but I think you have a chance. Then all this will be over."

"You want Zeus to die?" I questioned. "You want me

to murder him?"

"Perhaps not in cold blood but in self-defense… I don't see anything wrong with that. At the end of the day, someone is going to die, and I would hate to see it be someone innocent. Zeus has done many horrible things in his life. Yes he saved us all from Kronos, but he has committed almost the same crimes as his father. If you don't stop him now, then his tyranny will never end."

I frowned but knew what he was saying. It was the prophecy, after all. Perhaps it was his turn to fall so that someone could take his place. Wasn't that what time was all about—changes, rises, and falls? Nothing was meant to last forever.

"Thank you for being a friend, Hermes. I really appreciate it even if you had to side with Zeus in the end. I don't blame you, and if I survive, I won't let Father punish you. Although, if I die, I can't promise he won't come after you."

"That's fair. I will have deserved it either way. I just pray that you will survive. Many of us do even if our hands are tied."

Hermes and I landed on top of the Acropolis among the ruins of the Parthenon. My mother had told me stories of how Athena was once worshipped there and how Athena and Poseidon used to fight for the location. I guess in the end, Athena was victorious.

Athena was nowhere to be seen, which I was glad for because I didn't want to have to battle any more gods. I didn't even want to fight Hermes. I stood next to him, staring up at the sky where my father and Zeus currently fought. Would they even realize I was down there? Would my father end up winning?

What if Zeus ended up defeating him? What if my father lost his life because of me?

I didn't even want to think about that. I couldn't comprehend him being in Tartarus for the rest of eternity—he didn't deserve it.

As we stared up in the sky, I heard footsteps come up from behind us. I turned, ready to attack whoever it was to find that it was Pothos and Mel. I was surprised they were still risking their lives for me. As I was about to embrace them, I noticed a figure behind them.

It was AJ.

This was all his fault. He was the one who suggested coming up to Earth. He used my emotions surrounding my mother to convince me to come up here. He waited for hundreds upon hundreds of years for the right chance to convince me. He lied to me—he used our friendship to get his freedom from the Underworld.

I felt the darkness inside me begin to take form. I wanted him dead—I wanted him to spend eternity falling in that pit of despair with all those who had done evil in this world, whether they be human or god.

I shot out darkness straight at AJ. It was the first time I had ever been able to focus on one target for my powers instead of taking everything out around me, for which made me thankful, otherwise my friends would have gone down to Tartarus as well. A dark black lightning exploded where AJ once stood. A moment later, he was gone.

Pothos and Mel just stood there, wide-eyed. I glanced over to Hermes, who was also surprised at the power that erupted from me and how it didn't take out everything else.

"Whelp," Pothos commented. "No more AJ."

Mel let out a sigh. "I was having so much fun torturing him too."

"And this, my dear Chrys, is an example of why you shouldn't exist."

We all turned to find Zeus standing there, a lightning bolt in his hand. The sky was still full of a monstrous rage, with lightning exploding every which way. Was this all the power Zeus possessed? Or was he still holding back?

Zeus went on as he stepped forward. "He shouldn't have been able to be killed—not with the immortality I bestowed on him. Only I should be able to end his life."

There was no backing out of this. There were no excuses, no. "You shouldn't have been able to give him life like you did. You claim no one should have the power of life or death, and yet you use that power all the time. It doesn't seem fair."

Zeus's lips turned up into a half smile, as if all this was entertaining for him. "Are you trying to say you want to overthrow me?"

I shook my head. "No, I was just pointing out how you have double standards for all the gods. You are allowed to do whatever you want, but if someone is shown to have the same power, then they aren't allowed to live. If no god is supposed to have this power, then wouldn't that mean you shouldn't have the power either? It's unnatural, after all."

He shook his head. "No, that is not how this works. I have this power to protect all the gods and lives on this world. This has nothing to do with the powers I possessed but for the acts you have committed. You killed Poseidon—you killed a god of Olympus."

"He tried to kill me, not to mention last time he tried to kidnap me. Oh, I forgot, a woman can't stand up for herself when men like you are around."

Mel clapped. Pothos appeared as if he were going to join, but Zeus shot them both a glare, and they stopped and looked away.

Zeus held up his hand. "Goodbye, Chrys. I'm sorry there is no other way."

As he readied his attack and light began emanating from his hand, Pothos, Mel, and Hermes took cover. I stood there, ready to use my powers against the attack. I summoned the darkness and was about to prepare it as a shield when Zeus suddenly fell back. The action made him lose his hold on the lightning and it crashed all around me. I felt part of it hit me in the leg and screamed in agony, as my darkness wasn't able to block it. As my eyes adjusted after the blinding light, I found my father holding back Zeus's arm. Hades's hand and arm were scorched and blackened from the lightning.

Father growled. "You will not hurt her as long as I am still breathing."

Zeus tried to pull his arm away, but my father didn't budge. "We have been fighting for hours, brother. You cannot defeat me."

"There is only one way to stop me from defending my daughter and that is for you to kill me as well."

Zeus shook his head. "No, I will not kill you, my brother. You aren't the one who deserves to die."

"My daughter does not deserve to die. You are just full of suspicion and worry because of what that soothsayer said. Do you not realize she manipulates you to do her bidding? If you weren't so paranoid, half the things pursuing you wouldn't even care you exist. They would just go on with their lives, but instead you are disrupting their lives and trying to destroy them. So of course they try to fight back!"

"That is not true. I have stopped many disasters by

heeding her word, and I don't believe anything she says is false!"

"Then you will have to kill me, brother, for I will not stop fighting until I am dead."

"So be it." Zeus held up his hand, and lightning began to form once again. Father didn't let go of his arm and used his free hand to gather darkness.

I shook my head. I couldn't let my father fight to the death because of me. I had to stop Zeus before he sent Hades to Tartarus. I was the only one who could stop Zeus now—I had to fulfill the prophecy once and for all.

Gathering up energy, I prepared to act.

CHAPTER 22

Huntley

Why did Charon always take forever for everything?

I mean, I understood when you had nothing else going on and had been alive for millennia, but right now time was of the essence, and he did not seem to be trying to hurry back to the entrance of the Underworld. And then he went on and on about Hercules and how he didn't stay in the boat at all times like he was supposed to, and then he felt responsible for him escaping the Underworld. He swears Hades didn't trust him after that, even though Persephone kept saying that wasn't true.

Let's be honest. I was ready to strangle him. It was taking much longer to get back. I wanted to punch something, but I knew better than to punch something on a boat, especially one on rivers such as these.

But seriously, at least fifteen minutes had gone by, and I could barely make out the entrance to the outside. Why was this taking so much longer? Why couldn't we just transport out of there?

Persephone was biting her nails at that point. I had never seen her nervous, like ever. I'd feel worse for her if it weren't for the fact half of this was her fault and because I was more worried about Chrys than anything. I was past the point of blaming her, but it made it so I didn't feel quite that sorry for her.

No, I was sorry for Chrys.

This was total bullshit. Hermes had acted like he was going to help us but then screwed us over right when we were going to get away with it all. Why would he betray us like that? He had helped us figure out how to keep Chrys safe or at least plot to get Zeus to not marry her. After everything we did, he went and stopped the last possibility of her getting away and being safe down there.

And Chrys didn't fight it.

I knew she was powerful enough to stop him, but she did nothing as he flew up and out of this place. She had to have cared for him more than she let on. If she didn't, she would have taken him out right then and there. Hermes had guarded her when she was in the

Underworld, so they must have become friends. It seemed to be that way when he found Hades and I plotting to get her free of the marriage.

But now he was taking her to Zeus, and we were stuck on this fucking boat that was moving slower than a fucking sloth.

I took a deep breath before I decided to bite Charon's head off. It wasn't his fault how fast the boat went. He was trying his best. It was telling since he hadn't tried to talk to us since Hermes took Chrys. He understood what was at stake.

"Charon, for the love of all that is holy, move this fucking boat faster! Don't you realize what is at stake? Don't you realize that Chrys will lose her life if we don't do something?"

Charon gave me a look but kept on steering the boat at slow speed. I clenched my fists.

"She'll be fine," Persephone whispered to what appeared to be herself more than me. "Hades is there. She will be fine. There isn't much we can do now anyway. Zeus is up there, and he will stop at nothing."

I sighed but didn't say anything as I knew it would just make matters worse. Although Hades was a powerful god, that didn't mean that Chrys was safe. Hades could keep his own against Zeus, that was for sure, but he had a soft spot for his daughter, and that was going to be his weakness in fighting Zeus.

Because all Zeus had to do was direct his lightning at Chrys, and Hades would step in the way…

Zeus wouldn't actually kill his brother, now would he? I mean, he always talked about how family was important to him, and yet was willing to kill his own brother? And Hades was also one of the original gods, which meant if Zeus killed him, he would be disrupting the order of things just like he claimed Chrys was doing.

Gods made no sense.

However, Chrys had killed Poseidon, so order had already been disturbed. Things couldn't go back to normal now. Who would take Poseidon's place? What god was capable of taking over the sea? I didn't know anything about the politics of that, but I knew it wasn't going to be pretty.

And what would actually happen if Chrys killed Zeus? Who would be in control? Would it be Hera? Would it be Chrys? Prometheus wanted the title, but he was long gone now. Whoever took Zeus's place had to be powerful and someone all the other gods trusted.

Those weren't things I normally thought about, but my mind was spiraling while this boat took forever to reach the entrance to the Underworld. I finally saw the grand doors that had led us inside. Now we could finally see if Chrys was still okay.

Once we'd reached the shore, Persephone grabbed

my arm and transported us back. I turned away from her and threw up whatever was left in my stomach. I didn't think I had anything left. Where was all this coming from?

Once I felt my stomach settle and popped another breath mint into my mouth, I took in what was happening all around me. It was strange when one was so hyper-focused that part of your senses were ignored. Now that I was scanning the area, I realized that humans were screaming and running away, trying to get away from the thunderous crashing coming from on top of the hill. Already part of the city seemed to be in ruins —as if Zeus and Hades had been going all out in their fight, like some kind of superhero movie. The wind and rain still poured, and lightning crashed around the city, with the biggest concentration coming from the hills. People didn't know what to do or how to act. I even saw some news reporters puzzled on how they would show what was going on without getting hurt themselves. It wasn't like any helicopters could fly in this.

The hill that Zeus and Hades were apparently on was clear across the city. There was no way we were going to run there, especially with all those people in our way. A few shoved past us, and I let out a sigh.

"We are going to transport up there, aren't we?"

Persephone nodded. "Yup, sorry."

I grabbed her arm, and we were transported to the top of the hill where ancient buildings once stood. I tried to remember what they were called, but history wasn't my strong suit. Nothing was, which was a miracle that Hades let me hang out around his daughter for as long as he did.

Nope, there was nothing left in my stomach. I was surprised I would still feel like vomiting with everything that was going on, but alas, I did. Then I could focus on the events in front of me.

Zeus and Hades were in the middle of the ruins, throwing attacks back and forth at each other. I didn't know what was worse to watch—this or when they were simply fist fighting. I felt this was much scarier, but the latter was a lot more entertaining. Hades barely leaped out of the way as Zeus threw a bolt of lightning straight at his chest.

This was nerve-racking.

Hades countered with dark power of his own, but Zeus was able to block both. By the looks of it, Zeus didn't seem to have been hit at all, but Hades's arm had been charred, as if it took the full force of a lightning strike.

What the hell happened while we were gone?

Glancing around, I found Chrys standing to the side, simply watching her father with undisguised fear. Darkness spiraled out of her, but it was out of control—

as if she didn't know how to focus it. It was apparent
she didn't want to get in her father's way, but she also
didn't want him to suffer. I felt she was calculating the
best move but still hadn't found the answer.

Someone placed their hand on my shoulder, and I
jumped five feet. It was Pothos with Mel standing next
to him.

"There's nothing we can do but wait. There is no way
any of us would survive one blow from either of them,
whether it be accidental or direct," Pothos explained.

I nodded. He had a point. It wasn't like we could do
anything, not with Zeus there and Hermes making sure
we didn't make a run for it. I realized with the two of
them there, someone was missing.

"Where's AJ?" I asked.

Mel smiled. "Chrys killed him in one shot. It was
rather spectacular, to say the least."

Damn, I wished I saw it. I bet Chrys was badass.
Right now, however, she looked like a scared child
watching her father fight.

I saw Zeus's eyes turn to me, and he smiled.

Oh. Shit.

In an instant, he appeared in front of me and grabbed
me by the throat, dragging me toward the center of the
ruins we found ourselves in. I felt like this just
happened a few hours ago. Oh wait, that's because it
did. I was just a stupid liability and should have stayed

out of sight. Stupid, stupid human.

Zeus held me up by the throat. "You surrender right now, Chrys, or your human husband is dead."

CHAPTER 23

Chrys

I watched as Zeus grabbed my husband and held him up by the throat.

I couldn't believe what I was seeing. When did Huntley make it back? Why didn't he hide? What was I going to do?

"Let him go!" I exclaimed.

My father stopped throwing attacks at Zeus, as he could also hit Huntley. We both watched him, careful not to do anything that may cause Huntley's demise.

"If you give up now, I will let him go and he will survive. You understand, right? He will be in Tartarus for an eternity—where he was destined to go all along."

My heart ached, knowing that was the truth. Huntley

hadn't been the greatest human, and if it weren't for the fact that I had found him before Charon did, he probably would have gone to Tartarus. It wasn't his fault though. His actions had to do with circumstances beyond his control.

Hades had to have known, as he could see the truth in everyone's soul. But he also saw how much I cared for him and let it slide. It made me start rethinking how souls were judged, but that was a problem for later. Right now I had to save Huntley.

My father took a couple of steps toward Zeus as his attention was on me, but Zeus noticed right away.

Zeus held up his hand and grabbed a lightning rod. "Ah, ah. Do not come a step closer or I will kill him."

Father frowned but stopped advancing. I could see his pained face as his arm must have hurt. I didn't even know how we were going to treat that wound. Turning back to Zeus, tears ran down my eyes.

"What do you want me to do?"

"I want you to make your father and everyone else leave the Acropolis right now. Then I want you to close your eyes and not put up a fight as I kill you. If you do all that, I will let your human live even if he has been nothing but trouble. I didn't think many humans like him existed anymore."

"Hey, you sound like my parents," Huntley choked out.

Zeus tightened his grip, causing Huntley to struggle more, grasping for air.

"Do as I say, Chrys, or he will be sent to Tartarus for the rest of eternity. And I will still probably kill you."

Huntley was the most important person to me, aside from my father. I couldn't imagine either of them not in my life—even if it was a life in Tartarus. If either of them died and I did not, I wouldn't be able to forgive myself. If they died and I died, I would know the torture they were facing and be in even more pain. But if I died and knew they lived, maybe I could face an eternity in that pit.

I nodded slowly. "Fine. I will do as you ask. Just spare him and everyone I care about."

"No!" Huntley was able to yell as Zeus held him tighter.

Zeus laughed. "This is why you shouldn't get attached to others—it will end up being your weakness. Lucky for me that your dearest is this weak and pathetic."

"You are wrong," I said. "He is not weak. In fact, I think he's the strongest one here. He is a human facing gods, and yet he does not run away. Could you say you would do the same?"

Zeus frowned but didn't say anything.

"Besides," I went on, "If I end up in Tartarus, I will be able to endure knowing they were all okay."

My father interjected. "Which shows me she cares about others more than you do, brother. Why can't you see she doesn't want destruction? Why can't you think of anyone but yourself?"

"You do not understand how much I care, brother! I care about all of you and the entire world! A world she could destroy if she wanted to!" He shook his head. "She has even killed our brother, and yet you keep saying she is harmless? Open your eyes to the creature you let live!"

I felt Father's power begin to rise. I rushed over to him. "Father, don't!"

He glared at Zeus. "I will not leave her to die. Even if you beg me, daughter. I will not let you die for some human."

Tears were falling down my cheeks. "I can't let him die, Father! He does not deserve Tartarus!"

"And neither do you!" My father came to my side and grabbed my arms. "I am not leaving you. Huntley knew the cost. We all knew the cost. You are not going to be killed by him. I will not let him take the last thing I love in all the worlds."

I looked over at Huntley. His eyes were wide, but he was mouthing the words "don't give in." I shut my eyes, trying to think of all scenarios where we could all be fine, but we were way past that. I didn't want anything to happen to the ones I loved—especially since the odds of me getting out of this alive were near zero. But if I could get my father to leave, and the others, then it would just be Zeus and me. Odds were, he wasn't going to let Huntley go until I was dead. However, if there was a way where I could get Huntley away from Zeus, I could fight him one-on-one and just hope that I succeeded in killing him.

But my father couldn't even take him down.

Was I stronger than my father? I didn't think it was possible, but if Zeus was so worried, then perhaps I was —perhaps I could take him out.

Opening my eyes, I found my father still staring at me. His clutched his injured arm, and I took a look at it. My own father was suffering dearly because of me. No, I couldn't let this go on.

"Please, I can't watch him die. I will figure it out. I promise," I whispered.

He stared at me for a moment and then sighed. "Fine, but I will not forgive any of them if something happens to you."

"Well, Chrys? What will it be?" Zeus questioned.

I turned to Zeus and nodded. "I will do as you ask. My father will take the others somewhere, and it will just be you and me. Now let Huntley go."

Zeus bit his lip, as if he didn't believe me.

"I'll uphold my end of the bargain as long as they leave."

My father didn't say anything as he walked over to Persephone and the others. They were all gone in an instant. Now it was only Zeus and me.

I turned to Zeus. The only sound now was the thunder above as lightning exploded throughout the clouds. The wind whipped around, causing my hair to go in all directions. These sounds were loud, yet it all felt so quiet.

"Well then, let him go," I said.

He shook his head. "That wasn't the entire bargain. Get on your knees and close your eyes."

I hesitated. I wanted to get Huntley out of the way so I could attack Zeus, but he knew that. I had a feeling he wasn't going to let him go until the end. It would be a very brief moment where I could attack. This was going to be close, and I could feel my heart quicken with every moment.

Getting down on my knees, I grimaced from the injury he had caused earlier. "I want to see him survive —I want to know you will hold up your end of the bargain. I cannot do that if I close my eyes."

"Chrys, I am a man of my word. No harm will come to your husband if you obey me," Zeus said as he took a step closer.

I let out a laugh. "Right, as if I could believe that. You hold grudges and don't think things through. I want to see my husband freed before I die."

Zeus watched me for a moment, then shrugged. "Fine." Zeus let him out of his grip around his throat but grabbed his shirt to keep him close by. "He's out of danger right here, as long as you don't try anything."

He was on to me from the start. I guess it was pretty obvious. Now I just needed to figure out how to do this without hurting Huntley. I had promised my father I wouldn't end this without a fight.

"Now, close your eyes. Otherwise I will think you are plotting something."

There was nothing else left to do. I closed my eyes and tried my best to listen to when Zeus prepared his attack and Huntley was out of the way—that is, if Zeus was really going to keep him safe.

I felt the energy increase around Zeus, and I could sense Huntley there as well. Huntley was slowly moving out of the way, knowing I wanted a straight shot. I started to call upon the darkness that surrounded me.

That was when I heard another set of footsteps.

I debated opening my eyes, as I didn't want to let Zeus know that someone else was there, but I also had no idea who it was. Was it someone on his side, or was it someone who was going to help me? It didn't matter as I needed to be able to defend myself.

So I called upon all the power I could muster and sent it straight at Zeus. I opened my eyes at the last moment to find my father behind him, attacking in the same manner. Zeus was able to block both attacks, and I watched in horror when he was unscathed.

He shook his head. "I tried to be reasonable, Chrys, but you have left me with no choice."

Zeus held up his hand, and lightning headed straight toward Huntley. I dived toward him, but it was too late. Huntley got the full blow of the attack, and I watched as he disappeared from this world.

"No! Huntley!" I screamed.

CHAPTER 24

Huntley

So this is what hell was like.

Honestly, I always imagined I would go to hell, so this wasn't a big surprise. I always thought it would be fire and brimstone, though, with a horned figure poking me with a trident. Well, I guess my afterlife did include a trident being pointed at me, but that was Poseidon, not the devil.

This hell wasn't like that. No, it was dark and I was falling farther and farther down. I couldn't see anything except the darkness that was this place. I could hear screaming from all the souls that fell around me, but I didn't scream. I wasn't afraid for myself anymore—I was afraid for Chrys and how she would soon possibly share this same fate. She would be all alone for eternity, and if I hadn't screwed this all up, she would have been fine.

Was it my fault that Chrys was in this mess? If we hadn't found the pomegranates and succumbed to the temptation of wanting to make love with one another, Chrys could have married Prometheus and none of this would have happened. Zeus would have believed them, and then we wouldn't be in this mess right now.

If I wasn't such a junkie, all this would have been fine. If I had convinced her going to Earth was a bad idea, it would have been fine. If I was a better friend, we would be laughing and playing around the castle like we used to.

I deserved being in hell.

Something in my heart knew that wasn't true, which surprised me. I always considered myself a pretty crappy person, but the love Chrys had given me taught me I could love myself. I was worthy, and I didn't need to suffer like this.

Except that didn't stop the fact that I was indeed going to suffer for an eternity.

Would I mentally be able to keep telling myself I didn't deserve this? Probably not. Eternity was a long time. In fact, I doubted I could even comprehend how long that really was.

I had to redirect my thoughts. I had to tell myself

why I was really here—and that was because of AJ.

At least he was down here suffering as well. He was the one who deserved all this. He waited centuries to betray her like he did so he could return to Earth. He was promised paradise, yet he'd rather go back to Earth. No he was suffering in Tartarus.

What an idiot.

I didn't understand why these gods liked Earth so much. It was something I agreed with Hades on—the Underworld was much cooler and more fun than that place could ever be. Well, that is, if you weren't falling into the pits of hell.

So I guess Earth was better than this part of the Underworld. Maybe. Usually.

It was strange to think that Poseidon was also down there, falling, just like I was. It kinda showed that gods and humans in the end weren't much different, or at least when it came to Tartarus. Also, he should have known what was going to happen when he went against Chrys. This was literally he and his bastard son's fault. If they hadn't tried to screw Chrys over, they wouldn't be falling like I was.

I guess I had an eternity to keep going around with that in my head.

The air down here was cold. It wasn't cold enough where I felt like I would pass out, but it was cold enough where I wished I had more clothes on. Did I even have clothes on? I couldn't tell because everything felt disoriented and I no longer knew where I ended and the darkness began.

Not to mention that my ears were starting to ring from all the screaming.

This was my life, or I guess death. Afterlife. Yeah, that seemed right. Would all this cause me to cease to exist? Would I lose my mind and just not be anything anymore? Would there come a point where I forget everything? I didn't quite understand what the afterlife was supposed to be like and what our souls really were. How could so many people fit in this darkness? Did this darkness go on forever?

I did not like all those philosophical questions that were appearing in my mind. I tried to ignore those thoughts when they came up, mainly with drugs. But now I had nothing except darkness. It was literal torture.

Oh right. I was in hell.

Suddenly I felt something grab my arm and start to pull me up.

Or maybe I had just turned upside down and what was up was now down. Was this what Alice felt like when she went down into the rabbit hole? Would I eventually reach Wonderland? How cool would that be?

I was definitely starting to lose my mind in here. How much time had passed? It seemed like years, but perhaps it wasn't. I was not going to last an eternity.

Now that I was focusing a little harder, I realized the feeling was the opposite of what it was earlier. Something was definitely pulling me up. Was it part of Tartarus? Was this darkness just the purgatory before actually being thrown into what my vision of hell was? I didn't know which was worse. The unknown was always more comforting and more scary at the same time.

I heard the souls around me scream as I was pulled through them. Sorry dudes, I don't know what is causing this. I am as helpless as you all are.

Then all of a sudden, I was out of Tartarus and above Hades's castle.

I looked up to find Hermes's large wings. He looked like a guardian angel right now, but I didn't consider him one. He had taken Chrys to Zeus after all.

But I kinda wanted to kiss him. As a thank-you. Maybe just a hug.

"What the fuck? Hermes?" I finally was able to get the words out of my mouth. I still couldn't believe what I was seeing. Was this a hallucination? Or was this really happening?

"That's me," Hermes replied.

"What are you doing?" I asked. I mean, it was obvious, but I still had to ask.

"Saving your ass."

"Okay, I guess the better question is why?"

"Because you clearly needed saving. And besides, it is the least I can do for Chrys. She didn't want you dead, and if it weren't for Hades, Zeus might have actually let you go."

That was fair. I didn't blame Hades though, as he was just trying to save Chrys. I would have done the same in his shoes.

"Now what happened after I died? How much time has gone by? Is Chrys still alive?" I asked.

Hermes shook his head. "I left right away, so it has only been a few minutes. As for if she is still alive… My guess is yes."

"Wait, if you can save me, why can't you save Chrys if she is killed by Zeus?"

He hesitated. "Because, well, she fell in Tartarus once… Something down there wants her. My guess is Kronos, the titan that sired Zeus and the other gods. I wouldn't be able to retrieve her once she was in his grasp, not without bringing about an apocalypse of sorts. The same goes for if any of the big three died. I can't get them down there with Kronos waiting…"

Of course there would be an apocalypse. I mean, why not? Why not make it more complicated than it had to be?

"Then we just have to kill Zeus first."

"Bingo."

"So you are going to help us?"

"No, I was just agreeing. I wouldn't get in the middle of that fight for anything. But I also didn't want you to spend eternity in Tartarus. I like your spunk. Life would be a lot more boring if you weren't around. And you don't deserve eternal torment."

I laughed. "And you are probably the first adult who has said I don't deserve hell."

"Well, I'm a god, not a human adult. But okay."

"You knew what I meant."

"I suppose. By the way, you are a lot heavier than Chrys."

I ignored the comment. "Just get us back to Earth please. We have to save her."

"I mean, I really doubt you will be able to save Chrys. You're a human. Speaking of which, the only reason I can take you back is because Zeus gave you eternal youth and because he just transported you here versus actually killing you. You are lucky I don't have to drop you off somewhere in the castle."

"Yeah, yeah, if I wanted commentary, then I would have Charon guide me to the exit. Now, hurry up and get us out of here."

Hermes made a little smile then flew up toward the door that led to the mortal realm.

CHAPTER 25

Chrys

Darkness engulfed my entire body, and I could feel every inch of my body give in to the power. Energy moved through all my veins and touched every part of me. This was my true power—complete and utter darkness—and I would not rest until Zeus felt my wrath.

Zeus stepped back with a laugh. "I see. Now we know what your full potential is. This is why you were prophesied to destroy me—this is why you can't live."

Hades stepped forward, pulling together what power he had left. "She is only doing this because you provoked her. If you would have just let her stay in the Underworld like she had been for thousands of years, then there wouldn't have been a problem."

A lightning bolt formed in Zeus's hands, and the clouds above roared with anger. I jumped to the side as lightning struck right where I was standing. I wondered if I could use the darkness to block his attacks now, as I had failed earlier. It wasn't something I wanted to find out the hard way, however. It was better to be safe than sorry.

I reached my hand out toward Zeus and summoned the power inside me to strike out at him. He leaped away, and my father tried to attack him before he could counter. Zeus rolled out of the way, but Father's attack clipped his side and Zeus let out a loud gasp.

"You can't win against both of us, Zeus!" Hades yelled. "So give it up and let me go home with my daughter!"

"Never!" Zeus raised his hand into the sky, and his eyes turned a glowing white. I watched in horror as dozens upon dozens of lightning strikes rained down on the battlefield. I had to use all my concentration and focus on dodging them as they danced around, even with my bad leg. I tried to ignore the pain that shot up through my body when I put weight on it.

As all my focus was on the sky above me, I forgot to keep an eye on Zeus.

Suddenly Zeus tackled me straight on. I struggled as I threw kicks and punches. He pinned me to the ground.

"Well, this scenario could have been a lot better if you had just married me. Instead, I will simply have to kill you."

I watched as large lightning strikes started to come barreling down toward us. I unleashed the dark power within me, and Zeus went flying off of me. I rolled to the side just as the lightning struck where my head once was.

Zeus stood up and appeared as if my attack hadn't even landed a scratch on him. How strong was he? Why did that do nothing to him?

There was a reason he was still ruler over all the gods. If he couldn't hold his own against more than one god, the other gods of Olympus would have overthrown him long ago. Especially his wife, Hera.

There was no possible way I could win this, was there?

I still didn't understand why it was prophesied that I would take him out. I understood that my power was strong and that no other god had such strength as mine, but so far it didn't seem like Zeus was having much difficulty countering my attacks. He easily deflected them or was able to jump out of the way. Even my father had hit him in the side, and although he yelled out in pain, it didn't seem to have slowed him down.

What the hell was I going to do?

Father tried to tackle Zeus, which surprised me the

most. I never could see my father as one who would tackle. He and Zeus squabbled as my father tried to pin him down. Lightning crashed down around them as Zeus tried to get Hades off him.

"Be careful, Father!" I yelled out as I hurried toward him, wary not to get hit by the lightning surrounding them. As I got closer, I saw lightning hit my father straight in the shoulder. He rolled off Zeus, his face in pain.

Zeus stood up swiftly and readied another bolt toward Father, but I was quick to tackle him. At that point, my body felt heavy and tired and I wasn't sure how much longer I could last.

Lightning came striking down around me, and I rolled up and hurried over to my father.

"Are you all right?" I asked as I helped my father up.

"I will be fine. Don't worry about me."

We turned to find Zeus standing back up and laughing.

"You two put on quite a show. But in the end, I will win."

Hades clutched his injured arm. "Then stop fighting if you think we can't defeat you! You make no sense, Zeus. Why can't you understand that we aren't after you unless you start attacking?"

"Because I don't know what you are planning in the Underworld! If I let you go, she could become stronger, and then I wouldn't stand a chance!"

Father shook his head. "So really this is just about how you are paranoid."

Zeus didn't answer but let more and more lightning start crashing down around us. How did he still have so much power? Was there no end to his energy?

If I could sit and focus, I would have been able to reach out and harness his energy to help my own, but I wasn't allowed to focus for more than a moment before he started throwing lightning in our direction. Father and I dodged the attacks, even with our injured arms and legs. I could tell my father was getting to the end of his rope, however, as his movements had slowed, and I worried he was going to get hit.

Deciding to try to unleash as much of my power as I could toward Zeus, I brought it all to my palms and let it manifest. When I felt that it was all I had left, I unleashed it straight at Zeus. Zeus held up his hand, and all of it absorbed into his lightning shield. I watched in disbelief as he stood there, unscathed. Perhaps I wasn't going to defeat him after all. I lowered my arms, feeling my body drain of all energy. This wasn't fair—none of this was fair.

Zeus stepped forward. "Is that all you got? Maybe I shouldn't worry about you overthrowing me."

I frowned. I did not like how cocky he was getting. I glanced at my father, who held his arm but still was ready to fight more. How long would this go on for? How long could Zeus keep this up?

Zeus raised his hand, and dozens upon dozens more bolts of lightning came shooting down from the sky. I dodged them as they came raining down upon me. My leg throbbed with pain and I grimaced.

"Just give up, Chrys! You aren't going to win this!"

I certainly wanted to agree and give up as my entire body was hurting and felt as if it were going to collapse. I watched as my father went to one knee and was breathing heavily.

Seeing him in pain made me want to give in and surrender. If he kept going on like this, I feared he wouldn't be able to recover.

As my focus had been turned toward my father, Zeus took the opportunity to strike. I didn't have time to react, but luckily my father noticed and tackled me. Neither of us were hit, luckily.

"Thanks," I said as I stood back up. I summoned some of the energy that was starting to come back and threw it straight at Zeus. He deflected it without hesitation.

What did I need to do in order to hit him?

Father nodded for me to go right, and I watched as he started running to the left. Hopefully if we were on both sides of him, we would be able to do something. It was our last option.

Zeus laughed. "That's not going to work, but I admire your efforts."

He sent lightning at both of us. I jumped but not quickly enough. Part of the bolt hit me straight into my good leg. I tumbled onto the ground and slid across the rock. I looked down at my leg that was now blackened.

Shit. I couldn't walk, not with both my legs like that.

I could heal it, I knew, but I needed time and to focus. I knew I didn't have either at the moment. I looked up to find Zeus throwing a few strikes at my father so he would be preoccupied for a moment, and then he turned to me. I watched in horror as he summoned all his power into his hand.

Zeus smiled down at me. "Well, Chrys, it was nice knowing you."

I shut my eyes, knowing that would be the end.

CHAPTER 26

Huntley

I wished Hermes would fly just a bit faster. I mean, I knew he was going as fast as he could, but I needed to know how Chrys was doing. Hermes said he would know if Chrys had died, so at least I knew she was holding her own right now.

At least that's what I hoped. I couldn't believe it if anything happened to her. It just wasn't possible. We had gone so far to have all this happen now. It just wasn't fair. None of this was fair.

Zeus wasn't fair.

I knew Zeus screwed over a lot of different gods over the centuries he had existed, but I felt this was going too far. I felt that a lot of the gods wanted Chrys to win so they didn't have to deal with his crap any longer. The problem was, no one trusted that she would win, so they hid. I couldn't blame them, as they didn't know her and they didn't want to risk their necks. I had been in Tartarus for a mere few minutes—I couldn't imagine what it would have been like for an eternity.

I still felt that all this was AJ's fault and was glad that he was suffering in Tartarus, along with his father. If they had simply not told Zeus, or perhaps left her alone, they would be fine right now. I didn't feel any pity for them and was glad they got what they deserved.

I could see the entrance to the Underworld again. It was strange to have seen it so many times today as we kept going back and forth to it. It wasn't normal and felt odd to see the gates to the Underworld again. I could even see Charon circling around with a boatload of souls. I wondered where they were headed and hoped they did right by the world.

Hermes landed, and I knelt down to take a quick breather. I had never held on to someone's arm for so long before and didn't realize how much energy that and falling in Tartarus consumed. I could use a good night's rest right about then, but there was still much more to accomplish.

I stood up and nodded. "Let's go."

"Right. Hang on."

I forgot—we would have to transport to the mortal

world. And I was going to get sick. Again. I hung on to him, and suddenly we were in Athens with the others.

Nothing was in my stomach anymore, but I still felt queasy. Maybe I was finally getting used to the feeling. Yay…

Peering up, it was apparent that Chrys, Hades, and Zeus were all still battling it out on the top of the hill. My eyes almost hurt from all the lightning striking. We were barely at the bottom, and all the humans in the area had vacated this disaster zone. I didn't blame them —if I had seen this when I was human, I probably would have made a run for it. There were a few stragglers, however, who had their cameras out and were trying to take video as the wind whipped around.

How much would the world change after this all hit social media? Would anyone even believe it?

Persephone, Pothos, and Mel were all staring up at the battle in horror and concern as well. Even as a human I could feel the power radiating off the area, although that could have just been the lightning.

I turned to Hermes. "Isn't there something we can do?"

He shook his head. "There is no way I'm going to go anywhere near that fight."

"Huntley, you're alive!" I heard a voice say behind me. I turned to Pothos bear-hugging me. They must have just noticed I was there as their attention was absorbed by the battle. "I thought you were a goner!"

I wrapped my arms around him. The fact that I was almost sent to hell finally hit me. I pushed back the tears, although complete dread and horror had now filled my mind. I could have been falling in that pit forever. I would have never seen these people—these gods I considered friends—ever again.

"I was a goner if it weren't for Hermes."

Persephone and Mel joined the circle. Persephone turned to Hermes. "Thank you. I understand you had to betray us and take Chrys, but you didn't have to risk your life going after Huntley. Maybe I will spare your life after all."

"It was nothing. Not the first time I had to dive into Tartarus, and I'm sure it won't be the last. Now what did we miss?"

Persephone shrugged. "They are still fighting. I don't know what else we can do. None of us are even remotely powerful enough to stop them."

I looked up at the Acropolis. She had a point. Even if I wanted to help Chrys, there was no way I could do anything other than get in the way. So should I stay here where it was safer, or should I go up and make sure she was okay? Zeus had already tried to send me to Tartarus as a way to defeat Chrys. I wouldn't put it past him to try once more, and Hermes saving me was likely a onetime thing.

I would just be a liability again if I went up there. She would have to do this on her own, or at least just with Hades. Hades had fought his brother before and had lost, but with both of them, it was possible they would succeed. They had lasted this long, so it was possible they would be able to defeat him, even if Zeus's power was a lot more flashy.

Persephone grabbed my hand and squeezed it tight. Her family was up there, and it was possible she wouldn't see them again. I squeezed her hand back, praying that by some miracle, they would make it out of there alive.

CHAPTER 27

Chrys

As I awaited to be struck down by Zeus's attack, I closed my eyes and grimaced. Moments passed and I felt nothing. Slowly I opened my eyes to find my worst nightmare had come true.

My father had jumped in front of the attack.

"No!" I screamed as I dived toward him, but it was too late. His body slowly turned into dust as it transported into Tartarus. In his last moments, he smiled at me, as if he was happy that I had survived.

Tears ran down my face as I stared at the empty space that was once my father. First Huntley and now my father were in Tartarus to be tormented for all of eternity. I couldn't believe it—I couldn't accept it.

Zeus appeared as surprised as I was that my father dove in front of the attack. He also let out a scream as he reached out to where his brother once stood.

"Brother! No!"

There was nothing we could do as his body was now dust. I couldn't believe what I was seeing. This wasn't possible—this just wasn't possible. My entire body started shaking. I had lost all control—I couldn't imagine a life without my father. The world no longer mattered.

All I could see for the future was death for everything that had ever existed. Nothing deserved to live—not when everything that had brought joy to me was gone. I had let them down. I had let them die. What was the point of this world if the most pure and caring people would have to suffer for an eternity?

I let out a bloodcurdling scream.

Zeus did his best to try to block the energy that came exploding out of me. I watched as he threw lightning strikes at the darkness and at me, but it didn't do anything to stop me now. The prophecy he so feared had now come true. It was his fault I had succumbed to this power, and he deserved to suffer the consequences.

Zeus didn't stand a chance as everything came pouring out of me: all my power, all my will, all my soul. He started to turn around to run, but I didn't give him the chance. I expanded my power, and he vanished even quicker than my father. He now suffered the same fate as them—a fate he deserved.

But I couldn't stop there. No, everyone needed to pay —everyone who let this happen—everyone who stood by and let Zeus do whatever he wanted. They feared him and now they would realize that they should have feared me.

I became the darkness. I became death. This world didn't deserve the life the gods had given it. It was filthy and full of those who deserved Tartarus. I wanted to make a clean slate—I wanted to tear it down once and for all. Then and only then could this world be as beautiful as it was meant to be.

The darkness pulsed out of my heart and expanded slowly. It drew from the negative energy of my soul. It drew upon my anger and resentment. All of it would pay for the injustice that was done.

My father had done nothing but protect this world and those who had died. He cared about each and every soul that passed and came to his realm. He ruled with kindness, and yet he was killed by a god who only cared about himself. It wasn't fair—none of this was fair. None of these gods, none of the humans or creatures ever thanked him. None of them cared.

Now they would feel the wrath of his daughter—the only person who understood what Hades had gone through for all these centuries.

My power pulsed past the Acropolis and moved its way through the city of Athens. This would be the first of many cities to come. I couldn't let any of them stand. All of it would be destroyed and sent to Tartarus where it belongs.

All I felt were plant life forces being destroyed as all the humans and gods had vacated the area. It didn't matter, as those plants would give me enough power until I reached the parts of the city where the humans hid. With each life, I would gain more and more power, and then I would be strong enough to take out all of Olympus. The gods up there deserved it after treating me like an abomination—after treating my father as if he were a wretched beast.

If they only showed me kindness and compassion, then things wouldn't have turned out this way. If they had just understood that I wasn't going to hurt them in the beginning but just wanted to be accepted, then it wouldn't have come down to this. This was their own undoing—this was because they feared the unknown instead of trying to understand it.

It was because they didn't think of anyone but themselves.

I should have done this long ago, then I wouldn't have lost my father. I should have unleashed this on Zeus the moment I had the chance. Now it was too late, and my father and my husband were dead.

And so the rest of the world would meet the same grim fate.

CHAPTER 28

Huntley

What. The. Hell.

Something wasn't right. Darkness had exploded from the Acropolis and was growing by the second. No lightning was apparent any longer, and the air felt cool —as if it were filled with death.

It felt like Tartarus.

Did Chrys finally do it? Was she able to defeat Zeus and send him down to the depths of hell? And if that were the case, then why did it seem as if the darkness was growing? Didn't she realize she could stop? Unless her power was going out of control like it used to in the Underworld, and if that was the case, how were we going to stop it?

Persephone collapsed to the ground. "Hades…," she whispered as she clutched her heart. "No…"

I couldn't believe what I was hearing. Was Hades dead? Did Zeus kill him? I peered back up at the hill. It made sense if that was what happened and had caused her to erupt. She had unleashed all her power and more than likely took Zeus out.

The only problem was the darkness was getting larger and destroying everything in sight.

It was like all the time in the Underworld when she lost control of her anger, except far worse. She had just lost her father, and he had been sent to Tartarus. He was falling forever in that void. I didn't even want to think about it.

I could understand her anger and understood why she was letting it all go. Her father had just been killed right in front of her eyes, not to mention I had been sent to Tartarus. She didn't know I survived and probably believed everything needed to be destroyed. Although completely different circumstances, I felt I could relate in a way, as I had destroyed my own world with drugs. She, however, had the power to literally destroy everything due to her anger.

I had to stop her.

The problem was, I had no idea how I was going to get close enough to pull it off. The moment I touched that darkness, I knew I would be sent back to Tartarus.

There had to be a way around it all—there had to be a way to get her to notice me and snap back to reality.

Glancing around, I found Pothos, Mel, and Hermes all staring at the darkness just as I was. They didn't run, knowing that this would be the fate for everything. All the world would be destroyed soon, and they were just sitting back and watching the show. As I saw Hermes standing there, his wings still visible, a thought occurred to me.

"Hermes, can you fly over this?" I asked.

He studied the darkness. "I can… but I'm not sure if your plan will work. It seems the darkness is radiating straight out of her, and the moment it touches you, you will be sent back to Tartarus."

"I have been hit by it before and wasn't sent straight there. Perhaps I can knock some sense into her before I turn to dust," I explained.

"I think this is a bit stronger than what her power had been before. I can't make any promises of this succeeding."

I shook my head. "It doesn't matter, now does it? She is going to kill us all either way."

Hermes shrugged. "I guess that is true."

Persephone still sat on the ground, tears running down her face. She had lost her love—a love that had lasted centuries upon centuries. Although they had fought quite a lot, her heart still loved him, and now he was suffering for an eternity. I felt bad for her. I felt bad for Hades. But I knew stopping Chrys would be the only way to make it better—it would be what Hades wanted. He wouldn't want his daughter to destroy everything.

I turned to Pothos and Mel, who simply nodded. They knew what I was about to do and that it would be the only way to save the entire world. No pressure.

Hermes grabbed my wrist, and soon we were up in the air. I looked down at the city that was still standing. Any humans who had been close to the hillside were running for their lives as this dark wave started to descend into the city. Trees, bushes, and flowers instantly died when the shadows overtook them. I didn't see any human get absorbed yet, nor did I want to. Once I snapped Chrys out of this, she would regret anyone she murdered, other than Zeus of course. That is if I could stop her.

I thought about Chrys and what she must have been going through. This wasn't fair to her. None of this was fair. I understood why she was exploding like this, but I couldn't watch her destroy everything even if the gods had betrayed her. There was so much life on this planet that had nothing to do with what happened. It took me a long time to understand that as well, as Chrys had taught me to care about others. Now I would be returning the favor.

We were getting closer to where Chrys was unleashing her power. I had never seen or felt anything so horrific. Even in Tartarus the air didn't feel quite this stale. It was as if I was feeling death. It reminded me of when I died and in my last moments this feeling coming over me. It made me have flashbacks to the moment, and I started to get queasy. I focused on Chrys, and the rest of the world for that matter. I had to do this—I had to save them all.

Once we were right above Chrys, Hermes let me go, and I braced myself to tumble across the ground toward her. However, Hermes was right, once I hit the growing darkness, it took all my strength to stay conscious.

I could feel my body and soul being ripped apart, trying to be sent to Tartarus. I prayed, however, that I would survive so I could save this world—so I could stop this darkness. It was as if something from another dimension or plane listened, and my body stayed in this world so I could run to Chrys. Her eyes were black, and it was if she wasn't seeing anything around her. Dark marks streaked across her skin, and wounds covered her legs.

I took a deep breath and wrapped my arms around her.

CHAPTER 29

Chrys

Something had wrapped itself around my body. I couldn't see what it was as darkness had filled my sight. But I felt like I knew what it was. I knew I had endured this feeling before.

Then it hit me— it was Huntley.

How was he back on Earth? Zeus had sent him to Tartarus—I had seen it with my own eyes. No, this wasn't possible. There was no way he was still alive.

Yet I knew these arms. This had to be Huntley. And if he stayed around me any longer, I would kill him. No, I had to stop. I had to stop all this for Huntley's sake.

I couldn't bear to lose him again.

The problem was, the darkness had complete control

over me by now. It wasn't like before where the
darkness was barely controlling me when I got
emotional. No, this was all my power unleashed at
once. There was no way I was strong enough to stop it.
There was no way I could regain my control. I was past
the point of no return.

Huntley didn't let go. He was willing to risk his life
for me.

No, I couldn't let him die. I was stronger than this
power. It would obey me.

Huntley was weakening, I could sense that. How he
was able to hold on for this long, I had no idea. Were all
the stories about true love being the all-powerful shield
against destruction true?

It didn't matter at this point. I had to stop this
destructive power.

Focusing more and more on my powers, I thought
about my time on the island with Prometheus and Circe.
Circe didn't focus on teaching me how to destroy things
but more on how to bring life to that which was dying. I
focused on that power. I focused on everything that was
dying around me and the soul force that kept it all
connected. There had to be a way to bring it back to
life. I was not only the daughter of death, but I was the
daughter of life as well. I focused on the force that kept
everything alive around me and worked to make it
larger than that which was destroying it all. It was like a

light that was breaking up the shadows, and little by little, the darkness melted away.

I opened my eyes to find the Acropolis covered in vegetation, with rabbits and birds and butterflies dancing around. I had done it—I had stopped the darkness from taking over.

I collapsed to the ground, tears running down my face. I had almost destroyed all this. I had almost destroyed the love of my life.

He fell down next to me, wounds from the darkness covering his body but otherwise fine. I would be able to fix them eventually, but my power was nearly depleted.

I put my hand on his cheek. "You're alive. How…?"

Huntley shrugged. "Hermes picked me up. Said he owed you."

I wrapped my arms around Huntley and held him tight. He was alive. I had one of the things in my life I cared about returned to me. He felt warm, and I thanked the gods that I hadn't killed him a second time.

I started bawling in his chest, and he held his arms around me tightly. My father was gone and there was nothing any of us could do. It was all my fault. If I had only unleashed my power sooner; if I had only learned to harness it so I could save him.

Huntley kissed the top of my head. "Take all the time you need. I'm here for you."

I heard footsteps and turned to find Pothos, Mel, and

Hermes ascending the hill. Hermes had a soft smile on his face as he saw Huntley and me. Pothos and Mel mainly appeared relieved that I hadn't destroyed the world.

Behind them, I saw my mother. I stood up, and we both just stared at each other for a moment. I knew she understood what happened, and I didn't know what to say. It was my fault that Hades was dead.

She held out her arms, and tears ran down my face as I hurried to her and started crying in her arms.

"It's all my fault. I'm sorry!"

She stroked my hair. "No, it's not. He knew the consequences. It is no one but Zeus's fault. Understand that, all right? None of this is your fault."

I cried in her arms for what felt like an hour. Huntley stayed close by while the others went to report what had happened. I didn't know what I was going to do next, but at the moment, I knew I just needed to let out all the tears that I could as whatever was coming next would take all my mental strength.

CHAPTER 30

Huntley

Days had gone by since the death of Poseidon, Hades, and Zeus. Chrys had become the queen of the Underworld and now ruled over the dead. She had become rather quiet and reserved, but I didn't push her. It would take her some time to mourn her father. He had cared for her for centuries—I couldn't even imagine what she was going through.

The funeral for the three gods was held on Olympus, and I was actually allowed to go as I was the husband of the queen of the Underworld now. I wasn't quite sure what that made me. Maybe like prince of the Underworld? Or was I just still some human? It felt weird to think that, but that was how I was announced at the funeral.

Everyone dressed in dark robes as incense was burned in the great temple that stood above Olympus. No one seemed to be mad at Chrys, as they understood she was protecting herself and the fact she almost destroyed the entire world and was powerful enough to destroy any of them. There were whispers of her power and how they all feared her and how technically she was the most powerful of all and should rule Olympus. If Chrys heard their gossip, she was ignoring them. I doubted she wanted to rule over Olympus and preferred the Underworld where her father raised her.

Persephone was free from coming to the Underworld. She and Chrys hadn't really talked since Hades's death, and I felt that they were each taking their time to come around to each other. A lot had happened—a lot of things that could have been stopped. They didn't seem mad at each other though, and for that I was thankful. They just needed time to adjust.

Chrys was standing in front of the statue made of Hades, staring at it as if she were thinking about him. A resinous incense burned that felt warming and almost sweet. I stepped up beside her and waited for her to say something.

She closed her eyes, and I watched as a tear fell down her face. After a moment, she turned to me and a little smile appeared on her face. "Thank you for coming up here with me."

"Of course. I wouldn't leave you to do this alone."

She glanced around. "They think I should take over Olympus, but I want to stay in the Underworld."

I nodded. "Whatever you want to do."

"They fear me here."

I didn't say anything because, well, they did. Everyone feared her—she almost destroyed everything. Most didn't come around to talk to her but rather kept their distance. All the gods were here, even Circe and Apollo. Since Zeus was dead, they didn't fear repercussions, and it didn't seem that Chrys really cared to get revenge on them. They didn't hurt her, they simply went along with Prometheus's plan.

Prometheus hadn't been seen since the battle, where he was an eagle and flew off in the opposite direction of Chrys. I wanted to find Prometheus and give him a little piece of my mind, and fist, but Chrys didn't really care. She understood why he did what he did, and in the end it probably saved her life.

I wrapped my arms around her. "I will always be there for you, no matter what."

She rested her head on my shoulder. "Thank you."

CHAPTER 31

Chrys

I peered down Tartarus as the souls of the damned rained down into the darkness. Everyone sent to Tartarus deserved it one way or another.

Except my father.

Tartarus was a never-ending pit where Kronos and the other titans were sent to during the early battles on Earth. This place was made for them, and it was only later when humans started disobeying gods that they were also thrown in this massive pit. It really all boiled down to the fact that if Zeus didn't like them, down into the pit they went.

And now Zeus was down there as well.

For humans it was just an endless darkness, but for us

gods, and I assumed titans as well, it was much more than that. Kronos had a completely different torture awaiting any god that was sentenced to death—I could feel it.

So there was only one thing to do: I had to figure out how to free my father from Tartarus.

I turned back to the palace and made my way to the throne room. I now had my father's duties and powers over the dead. I had a lot of work to get done, just as he did.

But when I wasn't working, I was searching every library, every story, every rumor on how to break someone free of the prison that was Tartarus.

Stepping up to my throne, I sat and looked down upon my world. This seat would only be temporary.

I would get him back.

***

To be continued in *Queen of the Underworld: Tartarus* coming July 2021

THANK YOU READER

Thank you so much for reading! Readers like you make it possible for authors like me to write stories! If you could spare a moment and leave a review on Amazon, Goodreads, BookBub, and wherever you like to buy books, that would mean the world to me! It really helps authors like me to succeed in the publishing world.

A big thank you again for your patronage. I hope you will check out the sequel duology *Queen of the Underworld* coming July 2021!

ACKNOWLEDGEMENTS

I want to thank everyone who made this novel possible. A big thank you to my editor Justin and Annie who hopefully hasn't gotten sick of reading my stories yet. Thank you to Biserka Design for the amazing covers for this series! I love them lot! A special thank you to Dr. Almira Poudrier at ASU for answering my questions about Greek Mythology as things get weird and confusing and even more weird. And, lastly, thank you to my husband and parents who are always supporting me.

ABOUT THE AUTHOR

Dani Hoots is a science fiction, fantasy, romance, and young adult author who loves anything with a story. She has a B.S. in Anthropology, a Masters of Urban and Environmental Planning, a Certificate in Novel Writing from Arizona State University, and a BS in Herbal Science from Bastyr University.

Currently she is working on a YA urban fantasy series called Daughter of Hades, a YA urban fantasy series called The Wonderland Chronicles, a historic fantasy vampire series called A World of Vampires, and a YA sci-fi series called Sanshlian Series. She has also started up an indie publishing company called FoxTales Press. She also works with Anthill Studios in creating comics through Antik Comics.

Her hobbies include reading, watching anime, cooking, studying different languages, wire walking, hula hoop, and working with plants. She is also an herbalist and sells her concoctions on FoxCraft Apothecary. She lives in Phoenix with her husband and visits Seattle often.

Feel free to email her with any questions you might have!

danihootsauthor@gmail.com